Not What I Signed Up For

FINDING FAITH WHEN ALL YOU FEEL
IS FEAR

Shannon Anderson

CrossLink Publishing
RAPID CITY, SD

Anderson/CrossLink Publishing
1601 Mt Rushmore Rd. Ste 3288
Rapid City, SD 57701
www.CrossLinkPublishing.com

Ordering Information:
Quantity sales. Special discounts are available on quantity purchases by corporations, associations, and others. For details, contact the "Special Sales Department" at the address above.

Not What I Signed Up For/Shannon Anderson. —1st ed.

ISBN 978-1-63357-404-5
Library of Congress Control Number: 2021937894

This book is dedicated to Emily,
with much love.

Chapter 1

Dad handed Mom the police scanner, kissed us all, and headed out to his squad car under darkening skies. Mom lit a few candles and opened up the old wooden trunk we used for our coffee table.

"How about a game of Chinese checkers, girls?" Mom asked.

Playing games during power outages had become kind of a family tradition for us. I was fine with it—unless it was one of those times Dad had to go out because of tornadoes, like now. I wasn't really in the mood.

But my little sister, Maddie, ran over from the couch. "I get green!"

I stood up. "Is Dad going to be okay? Shouldn't we open up the crawl space?"

"Right now it's just a tornado *watch*," Mom said. "Em, you know Dad has to go out and help check the sky for funnel clouds. He'll be okay. It's just a precaution."

"Mmmm, that candle smells like sugar cookies!" Maddie said, seeming not to have a care in the world.

Mom gave Maddie the green marbles and I watched as she started placing them on the wooden board.

"What color do you want, Em?" Mom asked.

Hearing her but not really listening, I tapped the weather app, then walked toward the window to stare up at the sky.

"Emily?" Mom said.

"What? Oh, I don't care—whatever." *How can they even think about playing a game right now?*

After Mom placed red marbles on her point of the star, she put some blue ones on the triangle in front of me.

The last marble didn't even make it to its starting place before Maddie said, "I'll go first!" She picked up a green marble and jumped it over one of her others.

Mom took a turn, and then I sat on the floor and moved one of my marbles.

As the game continued, I looked around the living room. Lucy, our hyper papillon, panted as if she also knew it shouldn't be family game time.

"Hey," I said. "Where are the cats? If a tornado tears through here, we have to find the cats."

Mom glanced around, then called out toward the dark hallway leading to the bedrooms, "Tucker . . . Buddy! Here, kitty, kitty, kitty! Here, kitty, kitty, kitty!"

In seconds both cats came running toward us, tails straight up in the air, with a little curl on the ends.

"Well, Em, they expect some kitty treats now. Can you take the flashlight and grab some out of the basket?"

I blinked and then looked at my sister. "Maddie, you go get them. I don't want to go down that dark hallway."

"Nope!" she said, then pushed her glasses farther up her nose. "It's my turn again. You're the one that wanted the cats in here."

Glaring at Maddie, I snatched the flashlight from Mom and ran to the kitchen closet. On my way back I stopped to check out the window again. Toward the field the greenish sky had a big gray wall of clouds to one side. The wind whipped the gourd birdhouse in our tree around like a Barbie shoe in the vacuum canister. Rain drummed a warning on the windows and roof. A huge branch from the neighbor's tree crashed down onto the road.

Then the terrible scream of the tornado siren cut through the roar of the wind. Goose bumps broke out on my arms and neck.

I turned and hurried back to the cats with the treats. As they gobbled them up, I handed the flashlight back to Mom. "I told you we should've opened the crawl space!"

With all the excitement, Tucker and Buddy scattered immediately after finishing their snack. Tucker ran toward Maddie's room, and Buddy headed for Mom and Dad's bedroom.

Giving me a forced smile and shrug of her shoulders, Mom blew out the candles, grabbed an extra flashlight, and picked up Lucy. "Let's go, girls," she said.

We all rushed to her bedroom closet, where Mom handed me Lucy, then kneeled down to pry open the carpeted wooden top of the crawl space.

At the same time, Maddie tried coaxing Buddy out from under the bed, but he stayed put. I called out to Tucker while Mom lifted off the lid.

Then Mom looked up and pointed toward the bedroom door. "Shut the door so Buddy doesn't try to leave," she said.

I ran and shut the door, then turned back to see Mom helping Maddie step down onto one of the upside-down buckets we kept below. I grabbed Mom's arm with one hand and held on to Lucy with the other when she reached to help me climb down.

"What about Tucker?" I asked.

"That old cat knows something's up," Mom said. "He's probably found a good spot in the house."

Yeah, I thought, *he's probably heading back to the top of his cat tree—by the window! Not exactly the safest place during a tornado.*

I sat on a bucket, set Lucy down, and checked the weather update again. As I expected—the update now showed a tornado *warning* rather than a *watch.*

Mom pulled the lid over the opening, then sat down and turned on a battery-operated lantern we always kept there. Finally, she flipped on the switch for the lightbulb in the crawl space so we'd know when the power came back on.

"Can I go grab our game and bring it down here?" Maddie asked.

I looked at her. "Seriously? A tornado could rip through at any minute and you want to play a game?"

"I'd rather die having fun than be stuck on a bucket with nothing to do."

Her comment signaled the part of my brain that takes over when I worry. I sniffled and felt a few tears break free. One blink and the floodgates were going to open. Even Lucy was shaking.

Mom put a hand on my arm. "No one's going to die. We just have to sit and pray for the storm to pass."

Bending my head, I shot out a quick prayer. *God, please make this weather clear up and bring Dad back home safely.*

As I reached to wipe my dripping nose, Mom's phone dinged. My head jerked toward the sound. "Is it a text from Dad?"

"Yep! Oh . . . he . . . he said a tornado touched down out by the roller rink. It ripped the roof off of one building and damaged two others."

Gasping, I tried to stand up, only to hit my head on the floor of the closet. Now my head throbbed and my tears were streaming even worse than before. I plopped back down onto my bucket, a prisoner in the crawl space, surrounded by probably a million spiders, about to have my house ripped apart. Dad needed to come home—now!

Mom touched my arm again, then closed her eyes and bowed her head. She was praying, which obviously hadn't worked when I tried it.

Chapter 2

When the lightbulb came on less than an hour later, we cheered. I rechecked the weather app and Mom texted Dad. The storm had passed through and out of our area. Mom gave us the all-clear to climb out of the crawl space, and we did a quick walk through the house, looking out the windows to see if we had any damage. Everything looked okay, and both cats had made it through, so we headed to the kitchen to make dinner.

Dad didn't come home until much later, but Mom let us stay up until he got there since summer break had just started. When he showed up, it looked like he had gone through a blender.

"The north side of town is a mess," he said, "and there are a lot of trees and branches across the roads in town. Lawn furniture was cartwheeling through the yards and streets. It'll be at least a week before people find their garbage cans. And they're saying we can expect more bad storms this week."

I didn't like the sound of that.

Mom glanced up at the clock. "Well, girls, I'm sure Dad wants to take a shower and crawl into bed, and you two need to brush your teeth and do the same. You have swim practice tomorrow."

I groaned. "Mom, I already told you I don't want to be on the summer swim team again this year."

She cocked her head to the side. "Your sister's on the team, so you might as well be swimming too. We'll have to go to all of the swim meets to see her swim. It'll be more fun for you swimming than just sitting and watching her."

"Hmph. No, it won't. I'm fine with hanging out until it's over and NOT having water go up my nose or looking stupid in my goggles."

In Mom's mind I wanted to quit swimming because I never got first place, especially when my little sister came along and won first or second place all the time. That didn't help, true, but I mostly just got sick of hiding my eye.

Stupid strabismus.

My left eye crosses in toward my nose like a magnet when I take my glasses off. I had eye-muscle surgery in third grade, but it didn't straighten it out. Mom got me mirrored goggles so my eyes weren't visible, and then prescription goggles so my eye didn't turn in with them on. But who wears their goggles for an hour between events? There's no way I wanted to let people see me with my goggles off. I let that happen once in the locker room, and one of the first graders came up to me and said, "Your eye's crossed!"

Gee thanks, kid. You think I didn't notice?

"Most of your friends are on the team too," Mom said.

She wasn't giving up, so I gave it one more shot: "I just don't understand why you're making me swim."

"Honey, you quit everything when it becomes challenging. You stopped taking piano lessons when you couldn't memorize the songs anymore. You quit soccer because you said it made you sweat too much. With swimming you should just focus on growing and improving. Don't worry about how anyone else does. Besides, you're in the top of your age group this year, so you may be surprised with how well you do. Stick with it this one more summer. It's great exercise. Next year I'll let you decide if you want to stay on the team."

I clomped off to the bathroom. "That'll be an easy decision," I muttered.

Mom and Dad tucked my sister in and then came to my room. Mom kissed my forehead and said, "Good night, Em. I love you."

Dad stood at the light switch. "Night. Love you."

"Love you both too. Mom, will you please close my closet door?"

"Yep." She reached over and pushed the white folding doors shut. "Night."

As usual I lay there patiently while Mom and Dad walked to their bedroom. Once their bedroom door closed and clicked, I put my glasses back on, grabbed my flashlight, and began my bedtime check.

Sock-footing it out of my room to the front door first and then the back, I twisted each handle and pulled. Both locked. I crept back to my bedroom and returned my trusty flashlight to its spot on my night-stand. At last, armed with my bear, Brownie, I took off my glasses again, then slid beneath the puffy comfort-er on my bed and pulled it up to my chin. My smoke detector's red light glowed above me and my nightlight still worked. Check. Check.

Worries of starting middle school in the fall then filled my tired brain. What if I got lost finding my classes, and what if I couldn't remember my locker combination? And how could anyone possibly use the restroom at school with only four minutes between classes?

Chapter 3

The sound of clanging pots and pans woke me up the next morning. Snatching my extra pillow, I covered my head, trying to fall back to sleep. Not only had I worried about middle school and more tornadoes during the night, but then I got a nosebleed from wiping my runny nose so much. I really wanted all the sleep I could get, knowing what a busy day I would have. But the banging continued. Thankfully, it was soon replaced by the sizzles and smells of bacon, eggs, and buttery toast. Before long Mom yelled out to us, "Girls! Time to get up! You need to eat something before I take you to practice."

I walked out to the kitchen. After I'd started eating, Maddie strolled out to the kitchen with some serious bed head. She crinkled up her nose and squinted at me.

"Gross!" she said. "You have a big hunk of egg stuck in your braces."

I grunted and said, "Good morning to you too," then I jumped down from my barstool and headed to the bathroom to pick out the eggs. Why did I have to get braces? Between my crossed eyes, thick glasses, and metal mouth, I would be the biggest dork in middle school.

After Maddie finished eating, we took off for practice. Along with my other reasons for not liking it, swim practice also reminded me too much of gym class. I sort of enjoyed swimming, but I couldn't keep up with my friends, so I thought dance and theater were a lot more fun. Two of my closest friends, Hailey and Lauren, were the best swimmers on the team. They had broken the team record last year for the 100-meter relay.

At least I knew we could always count on the first practices being easy. The coaches normally talked for half the time, so we didn't have to swim very much. I would have my same coaches from last year, so I kinda knew what they expected.

When Mom came to pick us up from practice, Hailey called over to me, "Hey, Emily! My mom says you can stay over tonight. Call me later if you can!"

I forced a smile. "Okay, I'll let you know. Bye!"

Of course, Mom heard this and started in. "That sounds fun, Em! You should stay. Go tell her now if you want."

My brain began searching for excuses. I wrapped my towel around me, slipped my flip-flops on, and headed toward the doors. "Maybe," I said over my shoulder. "But the first play practice is this afternoon, and I'll probably be pooped."

Mom stopped right there in the parking lot. She obviously wanted me to see her big frown—the kind where one eyebrow went up and the other slanted down toward her nose. "Em, you're missing out on making memories with your friends. What if they stop inviting you?" She sighed. "You always come up with some reason not to stay."

We climbed into the van to go home, and I remembered back to the last time I tried to spend the night at a friend's house . . .

* * *

Lauren and I made a mess of her kitchen baking Christmas cookies, and then made a mess of our faces doing blindfolded makeovers. She laughed so hard I thought she might pee her pants!

"Oops!" she said. "Ha ha! I got more lipstick on your nose than your lips!"

"That's okay. You can call me Rudolph!"

We always came up with the craziest kinds of fun. But then bedtime brought the fun to an end. Once Lauren had fallen asleep, my imagination got the best of me. *I bet no one double-checked their locks. . . .When did they replace the batteries in their smoke detectors last? . . . I'm sure no one at my house checked the locks. . . . I hope Mom's curling iron and the Christmas tree are unplugged.*

There was no turning back. Once the worry set in, I couldn't relax enough to fall asleep. Staring wide-eyed at the ceiling wouldn't help. Forcing my eyes closed didn't work. Knowing this struggle would last all night, I dug my phone out of my bag and called home. The pink-and-yellow peace sign on Lauren's floor swirled a little as I stared down, waiting for my call to ring through.

One ring. Two rings. Three.

Each ring seemed longer than the one before. Mom would eventually answer and she would be disappointed.

"Hello?" answered Mom's groggy voice.

"Hi, Mom," I whispered. "Will you please come get me and take me home?"

"What? Emily . . . honey . . . it's almost midnight." She paused to yawn. "You've already made it halfway through the night. Can you read or pray to take your mind off things until you're tired enough to fall sleep?"

Didn't she realize that from midnight to nine in the morning amounted to a really long time to lie there, scared to death?

"I don't feel well, Mom. I'm sniffling and don't want to keep Lauren up. Please just come and get me."

She gave a heavy sigh, then whispered, "I'll be there in a few. Be sure to get your things gathered up and tell Lauren you're sorry."

* * *

Since that night I'd managed to not spend the night anywhere except my own room. But Mom wouldn't let up on the ride home: "Emmy, please think about going."

Lucky for me, Maddie interrupted and blabbed on and on about the swim camp forms our coaches had given us. "Mom! Can I go to swim camp this summer? It's at Purdue! They take videos of us swimming with underwater cameras, and we would stay in the dorm rooms. Kennedy and I want to be roommates."

Thankfully Mom switched her focus to Maddie. "It sounds pretty awesome. I'll talk to Dad about it. You sure you could make it three whole days away from home?"

She stared at mom with confused surprise. "What? Oh . . . yeah, sure! It'll be fun. They said we swim all day."

I shoved my form deep into my swim bag. No way was I going to *that*!

Chapter 4

Since there wasn't a lot of time between swim practice and play practice, we got to have fast food for lunch. That's one good thing about being really busy. I shoved some hot, salty fries into my mouth as we pulled up to our house. I changed out of my swimsuit and headed back into the kitchen with my play script.

"Mom, do we have a binder I can keep my script in?"

Having a mom who was a teacher always came in handy. She had just about any school supply you could think of around the house.

"Yep! Look in the file cabinet by the desk. I think there are a couple in there."

I opened the drawer to the filing cabinet. Bingo! I found a blue binder with cutouts of stars all over it. It was perfect. I used Mom's three-hole punch and got my script organized.

The best part of the summer for me was Children's Summer Theater. It was my second favorite thing in the world to do. Kids from fourth grade up to eighth grade got to be in it. This summer the play was going to be *Seussical*—kind of a mix of Dr. Seuss books, put to music. And there was dancing too! *That* was my very favorite thing.

Our dance studio in town went out of business after I had only taken lessons for seven years. Mom said it was too expensive and would be a pain to drive out of town to another studio with our busy schedules.

I had started dancing when I was really little. Ballet, tap, hip-hop, jazz ... you name it. I *loved* dancing. There was nothing like getting lost in some music and forgetting about everything else. Performing in dance was sooo much better than competing in a sport, where people are there to see who wins and loses. At a dance performance people are there to see you express yourself and experience the music with you. When you're born to dance, moving to the music just happens, like breathing and the beating of your heart. No one wins or loses. You can't do it wrong if you love it.

Soon enough Mom dropped me off at play practice. Since it was our first session, we went over a lot of rules, just like swim practice. Then we all sat on the edges of the pit and did a read-through of the script. Even though it wasn't the most exciting time, I didn't want it to end because I just knew Mom would again try to convince me to stay at Hailey's.

And I was right.

Right after she picked me up from the high school, Mom started right in. I sank into my seat in the van and laid my head back on the headrest.

"Emily, go ahead and call Hailey back. I can take you there after you pack a bag. Here's my phone."

Mom forgot a lot of things, but she never forgot a sleepover invite.

"I'm so tired, Mom, especially after this first full day of practices. Plus, last time I tried to stay at Lauren's house, I didn't make it, remember?"

Mom shook her head. "That was months ago. It's a good time to try again. Hailey's mom will get you two to bed at a decent time, knowing you both have to swim early in the morning. I'm sure you'll get some rest."

"Last night I stayed up worrying about more tornadoes and I had a nosebleed, so I didn't get much sleep. I need a better night's sleep tonight. What if I get a nosebleed at her house? That would be embarrassing, and I could ruin her pillow or blankets."

"Em . . . you should try spending the night at Hailey's. You can take your own pillow. You've got to get over this. Once you stay somewhere once, you'll see that there's nothing to be afraid of."

Mom came to a stop at a light and said, "Here . . . take my phone and call her."

She placed the phone in my hand, and my stomach tied itself in a knot.

I frowned, then muttered, "Fine."

I made the call. Hailey's mom answered on the first ring. "Hello?"

"Hi, Mrs. Lewis. It's Emily. Is Hailey there?"

"Hi, Emily! Hailey was hoping you'd call. Here she is."

Then I heard Hailey's voice: "Hi, Emily! Can you stay over?"

"Yeah."

"Great! And guess what? My brother got a trampoline for his birthday, so we can use it!"

"Oh . . . nice," I mumbled.

I felt like I could puke. *Those things are dangerous!* My cousin broke her arm on one. Hailey and her brother would be doing flips and all kinds of things, and I would just bounce up and down and up and down like a big baby. I couldn't do any tricks—and didn't want to.

"Well, you can come over as soon as you're ready," Hailey went on. "My mom ordered pizza and it will be here at dinnertime."

"Okay. I'm almost home from play practice, then I have to pack a bag. So . . . I'll see you in a little bit."

"Okay, great. Bye!"

"Bye," I whispered.

My eyes teared up as I put the phone in Mom's purse on the floor of the van.

"Oh, Em, you're going to be fine." Mom reached out and patted my knee. "Try to have a good time."

As soon I got home, I trudged in and stuffed my polka-dot, quilted bag full of my PJs, a flashlight, my toothbrush, and a fresh swimsuit and towel for practice in the morning. Then I sat on my floor clutching Brownie until Mom called for me from out in the kitchen.

"Ready, kiddo?"

I rolled my eyes. Like I had a choice. I got up, heaved my bag onto my shoulder, and followed Mom back out to the van. We drove to Hailey's in silence until we pulled into her driveway.

Then Mom smiled over at me, looking all hopeful. "I'll see you after swim practice in the morning. Love you!"

I forced a smile and said, "You too. Bye."

Chapter 5

I took my time walking up the sidewalk to Hailey's house. The front door opened and their beagle ran up to me, jumping and barking. Hailey's mom met me at the door and took my bag.

"Hi, Emily! You can go on out back and jump around on the trampoline with Hailey while we wait for the pizza to come."

I just nodded and said, "Okay, thanks."

As I moped my way around the house to the backyard, I thought how I really did love pizza—but even that didn't sound good to me. And I ended up being right about the trampoline too. Hailey and her brother could both do flips . . . and I just bounced. I told Hailey my stomach hurt too much to try flipping.

I finally felt relief when I saw a beat-up red car with a sign strapped to the top pull into her driveway—not because I was hungry, but because it meant the end to the trampoline torture.

I picked at my pizza as Hailey talked on and on about the volleyball callout she went to today. I wish she would have done the play with me again this year. Most of my friends were in the play last year, but a bunch of them decided to go out for sports this summer so they could be on the middle school teams.

Soon enough Mrs. Lewis started clearing away our plates. "You girls want some brownies for dessert?"

I perked up. "Sure! That sounds good."

"So how was play practice, Em?" Hailey asked.

"We just did our read-through. I can't wait to start learning the dances. The songs are really fun this year."

Hailey smiled. "I'll definitely come and see you in the play next month."

Mrs. Lewis gave us each a brownie on a plate and said, "Yes, Emily, let us know when you have tickets. The summer plays are always enjoyable to watch." She smiled down at us. "When you're done with dessert, you girls can go change into your pajamas and watch a movie if you want. Need to make it an early night with swim practice in the morning."

I nodded. "Thanks for dinner, Mrs. Lewis."

After finishing our brownies, we headed to Hailey's room to change into our PJs. Then Hailey picked out an old movie I'd never seen, and we watched it in her room while lying on sleeping bags on the floor. My parents would never let me have a TV in *my* room. The movie was about a boy left at home alone. A couple of burglars kept trying to break into his house. Just what I wanted in my head when I had to try to sleep in a strange house . . .

I wanted to hold Brownie but didn't want to look like a baby. Thankfully Hailey snatched her stuffed monkey off the floor when her mom popped in to say good night, so I pulled Brownie out of my bag. But I wished Mom were there to shut Hailey's closet door and say good night.

"Make sure you girls go to sleep after the movie," Mrs. Lewis said. "You have practice in the morning. Good night."

We both said good night, and then Hailey's mom flicked off her light switch and we went back to watching the movie.

I really hoped I would be tired enough to fall asleep during the movie, but I made it through the entire horrible thing. At least I learned a couple tricks to scare off robbers.

Hailey got up and shut off the TV, then slipped back into her sleeping bag. Her room seemed really dark now with the TV off, but at least a little light came in under her door from the hall nightlight.

She looked over at me and asked, "Are you going to swim for the middle school swim team this year?"

I didn't even want to do the *summer* swim team. I sure as heck didn't want to do the regular swim team. But I said, "Uhh . . . I might. I haven't decided yet." I figured that would hold her for a couple of months—until I didn't show up for the first practice. Most of my friends would be on the team, and the rest of them would be playing volleyball and basketball. I sighed within, wishing we had a dance team.

Hailey just nodded and then changed the subject: "Oh, hey, did you get the invite about the dance today?"

I shook my head. "Dance? No . . . I guess I didn't get invited. Where is it?"

"No, you're invited for sure, because it's for all the new sixth graders. It's at the middle school. Kind of a back-to-school thing for all of us to get to know the students from the other elementary schools, I guess. My invitation came in the mail today with my report card."

"Oh. I don't know if Mom even remembered to get the mail in today. We had a busy day with practices and adjusting to our summer schedule."

"We're supposed to dress up for it. Hold on." Hailey got up and went to her bedroom door, then looked down at me. "I'll be right back. I think the invitation's still on the counter."

I lay there, thinking how dark it was in her room. It was really quiet too. My stomach twisted, and I swallowed hard. I remembered my flashlight and dug it out of my bag, then turned it on, which made me feel a little better.

Hailey came back a few seconds later with a square card that she handed to me. I pointed my flashlight at it and saw that it had our mascot—the Bomber guy—and red and black lettering on it. Then I read it:

Bomber Back-to-School Bash
Mark your calendars for
Friday, August 8, from 6:30 p.m. to 8:30 p.m.
There will be a dance, cookies, punch, and lots
of fun!
Come dressed for success in your Sunday best.

I laughed. "Nice rhyme! What're you going to wear?"

"Oh gosh, I don't know. We have a couple of months to worry about that."

"That's true. So how was your report card?"

"A few As, a few Bs. How about you?"

"Well, I didn't see mine yet, but I think probably about the same." I actually was pretty sure I had all As, but I didn't want to brag.

Hailey nodded, then said good night. I shut off my flashlight and just lay there in the darkness. Soon I started thinking about Lucy and wondered where she would spend the night, since she usually slept with me in my room. Maybe she would sleep with Maddie instead.

I tried counting as high as I could. I was hoping it would bore me so much I would surely fall asleep. I almost made it to two thousand. Even though I can count way higher than that, I stopped. It wasn't making my eyes heavy.

I squeezed my eyes shut and tried to think about the play. The script seemed really fun. There was a lot of music and dancing. I bet that the costumes were going to be awesome. I smiled and opened my eyes. Since one of my parts was a tightrope walker, I would get to do a little solo dance on a pretend tightrope, holding an umbrella for balance. I couldn't wait to learn my parts! I should have brought my script with me to read.

Read! That's what I could do. I felt for my flashlight on top of my bag next to me and then crept over to Hailey's bookshelf. She had a lot of good books. I grabbed a couple and lay back down. Reading almost always made me fall asleep. This could work. I could feel it.

I started reading. The first book was kind of weird, so I tried the other one. I felt my eyes getting heavier and glanced over at the clock. Eleven fifteen. Then I noticed a weird shadow on the wall behind Hailey's nightstand.

It looked like some figure wearing a hat. It kept moving up and down randomly. I got up and looked out the window but couldn't see anything out there. I knew it was a shadow, but was it just the wind blowing a branch or was something out there making it move?

I looked over at Hailey. She was asleep. It was eleven thirty. Only about eight hours to go until everyone would be up and eating breakfast before we had to go to swim practice. I did feel pretty tired. Maybe I could sleep hard and not wake up until morning. That would be amazing.

Then Hailey's window air conditioner kicked on and drowned out any possible noises I would need to listen for in case someone was trying to get in the window or front door. I realized I was choking poor Brownie. I went back to my sleeping bag and tried reading again. I read several pages but couldn't have told anyone a single word on them. Then I started hearing a low rumble, and rain started pinging on the air conditioner. I remembered Dad saying that more bad storms were in the forecast. The room lit up for a second with a flash of lightning.

Oh gosh! What if Mom and Dad are sleeping right through this? I have to let them know it's storming and get home now. It could be a tornado again!

A huge crack of thunder made me about jump out of the sleeping bag. Lightning flashed and lit up Hailey's room again.

With a trembling hand I shook Hailey's shoulder.

"Mmm," she muttered but didn't wake up.

"Hailey!" I whispered. I pointed my flashlight at the floor in between our sleeping bags so we could see each other. "Hailey . . . can you get your mom?"

Now Hailey's head came up off the pillow. "Huh . . . what?"

"I think I better call my mom. My stomach hurts again, and I don't know if I'll be able to go to swim practice in the morning. I think I'll just have Mom come and get me now so your mom doesn't have to make a special trip in the morning to take me home."

"Oh . . ." She yawned. "Okay. Let me get the phone for you, then I'll tell my mom you're leaving."

Alone in Hailey's room I called Mom—and she didn't even seem to care at all that I was scared! She just thought I was being a big chicken. But even if I was, she should have been more understanding. She was the one who told me to try. I tried. I wouldn't want my kid to cry herself to sleep because I made her stay somewhere that scared her.

"Emily, it's so late. We're all in bed. You'll be fine. Just go to sleep and I'll see you after swimming tomorrow. Nothing's going to happen to you. You're just nervous about staying somewhere. Pray about it and try to go back to sleep."

Just then Hailey's door opened, and she walked in with her mom.

"No!" I said to my mom. "I just . . . feel sick. I can't fall asleep and it's storming. What if it gets bad again? Please come and get me. Hailey's mom is right here if you want to talk to her."

"What? I can't believe you woke her up too! All right, all right. I'll have Dad come get you. Get your things gathered and be ready at the door so everyone can go back to bed. We'll see you soon."

I turned to Hailey and her mom. "My dad will be here to get me soon. Sorry, Hailey. Sorry, Mrs. Lewis. I'm gonna grab my stuff and wait by the door."

I didn't know which was worse: being scared all night, or disappointing Mom and Dad again.

When Dad got there, he came up to the door looking more like he was there on police business to cuff and stuff someone than to pick up his own kid. When we got to his car, he didn't waste any time: "Emily, I just don't see why you have to be so scared about spending the night at friends' houses. You're lucky they don't make fun of you."

I took a deep breath and squished my eyes shut. My tears and nose started leaking all over the front of me. I brought my head down to my sleeve to wipe my nose. They just didn't understand. I really had tried to make it.

Back at home I tossed my bag on my bedroom floor and then waited for Dad to go to his room. I still had to check the doors before I could even think about climbing into my bed. A little after midnight I finally crawled into bed. I was so thankful to lie down in my own room, in my own house.

Chapter 6

D ad's little "pep talk" on the way home from Hailey's was nothing compared to what he and Mom had to announce when I saw them in the morning. Alone in the kitchen, I climbed onto one of the barstools with a spoon and a yogurt in hand. I was about to see if we had any granola to sprinkle on top when Mom and Dad both walked into the kitchen—clearly on a mission.

Mom started with the horrifying news. "Emily, you and Madison are great swimmers, and we think the Purdue swim camp would be a good opportunity for both of you."

My mouth fell open, but then I froze in place. *What? No! No no no! I'm not a good swimmer . . . and I'm scared to stay away from home. What part of swim camp is a good opportunity for me?*

Dad put his hand out to shush me even though I wasn't saying anything. "Maddie really wants to go, but we would feel better if you were there with her. Maybe you would enjoy swimming more if you were able to learn some new things to help you feel more confident about your strokes."

Now I closed my mouth and frowned. *In other words, maybe if you weren't such a terrible swimmer, you'd like it better!*

Then I imagined being away from home—*far* away from home . . . and far from Mom and Dad. My eyes started to sting and my heart started racing.

I focused all my attention on talking without crying, "Don't I have any say in this? . . . I don't want to go! . . . Why can't Maddie go with Kennedy?"

Dad shook his head. "Kennedy's going on her own. And we're sending both of you together. You have to get over this fear of staying places and realize you'll be okay. There are going to be other times that you need to stay over places for camps and lock-ins. Kids go to sleepovers and camps all the time and make it home safe and sound. Besides, you'll have your sister with you to keep you company."

I slid off my stool and slammed my yogurt down onto the counter so hard some of it flew up in the air. I stomped off to my room and *almost* slammed my door. I was already pushing my luck with the stomping, so I knew better than to do that. I did lock it, though.

I flopped onto my bed and let myself feel the anger burning through me. I couldn't even believe how cruel my parents were! It would be like making someone sit in a room full of snakes if she was scared of snakes. I grunted. *And what is the point?* That person would still be afraid of snakes—maybe even hate them worse.

AND the person would be pretty upset with the people that forced her to be there.

At least they left me alone until it was time for swim practice.

After I'd calmed down for a little while, I heard a knock on the door. "Em?" came Mom's voice. "It's time to leave for swim practice. Do you have your suit on and a towel packed? "

I didn't answer—I might have calmed down, but I wasn't happy. I just walked out of my room with my swim bag on my shoulder and kept right on walking out the door to the van.

Maddie and Mom joined me a few minutes later—and Mom wasted no time diving right back in: "Emily, I know you're upset. Swim camp isn't for a couple weeks, so please don't stress yourself out."

I groaned, then almost shouted, "I'm not stressing myself out! YOU are stressing me out. You and Dad don't understand! I don't want to go at all. There isn't one thing about it that sounds fun or good to me."

Mom started the van and pulled out. "Emily, we think you'll have fun at Purdue. You'll have amazing coaches . . . and the aquatic center there is awesome! You can eat at the cafeteria and pick whatever you want to eat. They have a big bookstore there, so we can give you money for a Purdue T-shirt or sweatshirt. And you can have money to order pizza at night too, if you want. Oh, honey, please try not to focus on the sleeping part, and open your mind to the fun you can have and the things you can learn."

And then it hit me. *The play!*

"But, Mom, I can't miss that much play practice!"

She looked over at me and smiled. "I already talked with the head director and said that we were thinking of sending you to a swim camp and that you'd miss three practices. He said it would be fine since you've done plays before."

"Great," I mumbled.

I decided I had lost the battle for now, so I just crossed my arms over my chest and stared out the window. Maddie jumped right in, enjoying every minute of being able to talk about going to swim camp. I just couldn't understand why it didn't freak her out to go to a giant college campus . . . with thousands of strangers . . . and be away from home . . . for three entire days and three nights!

I sighed to myself. Maddie was only eight years old. Where did she get her courage from? Why wasn't she afraid of tornadoes and robbers and boogeymen jumping out of closets?

Chapter 7

Hailey came up to me when we walked in for swim practice. "Are you feeling better, Em?"

I shrugged. "Not really . . . but Mom made me come."

We did a lot more swimming this time than the day before. They had us swim all the different strokes individually so they could see what we needed to work on most. I really wanted to concentrate on diving off the blocks and flip-turns, but the coaches said I had to work on my endurance—how long I could swim and keep a good pace. They also gave me a few pointers about my arms when I was doing the butterfly. For the most part I thought my strokes were pretty good. I was just slow.

When practice ended, Maddie and I went outside to look for Mom's van, but we didn't see it anywhere.

Then Maddie pointed over to a red car. "Dad's here to get us! That's why there's no van."

I pursed my lips. This was really strange. Dad should have been at work. Mom even said she would see us after practice.

We got in the back of the car and said hi to Dad, and he started driving home.

"Where's Mom?" I asked.

"She's at home."

"Why aren't you at work?" I went on.

He glanced at us using the rearview mirror, then looked back at the road. "Girls, you know the other day when we had a tornado touch down by the roller rink?"

Maddie and I looked at each other and both answered, "Yeah."

Then I asked, "Why?"

"Well, there's a place called Joplin, in Missouri, that had a tornado way bigger than that, and it destroyed a fourth of their city. It killed over a hundred people and totaled thousands of homes. There are a lot of people still missing and a lot of people hurt."

"Oh my gosh! That's bad," Maddie said.

"Yeah . . . but what does that have to do with you not being at work?" I asked—even though I didn't want to know the answer.

Dad took another glance at us in the mirror. "A few of the police officers that go to our church and some other guys are going to drive to Joplin and help. We want to try to find people who might be trapped or in vehicles somewhere off the road . . . or kids who may be lost or without parents."

"Okay. Is it dangerous?" I asked.

He shook his head. "The tornado's over. Now they just need lots of help. They have no power, and a lot of people don't have a place to live or anything to eat. We can bring them some food and water and help out any way we can."

"Where will you sleep?" Maddie asked.

"How long will you be there?" I asked before Dad could answer her.

"We'll sleep in a church there, but I really don't know how long we'll be gone. I just know that I'm leaving after I drop you girls off at home. Our group is meeting at the church and heading out once we have supplies gathered."

When we got home, Mom had loaded the van with cases of water, rolls of paper towels, garbage bags, food, bandages, and blankets. It was like our own Red Cross truck.

Finally, Dad got his bag from the house, put it in the van, and then gave Mom a kiss. After that he grabbed Maddie and me up in each arm. I could see tears in his eyes. I had been mostly fine until I saw that.

He said, "I love you, girls. I'll call when I can." Then he held onto us for a long time before setting us down.

Both Maddie and I had tears in our eyes, but Maddie could at least talk and say goodbye and "I love you, Dad."

My mind was way too busy for that: *What is he NOT telling us? If he's just going to help out, why is he so emotional? He never gets emotional.*

Dad hugged Mom one more time, then climbed into the van and pulled out.

I finally found my voice. "Love you!" I called out.

"Love you, Dad!" Maddie yelled.

We turned and followed Mom back into the house. Mom was so busy gathering things for Joplin that she hadn't had time to make lunch. "Girls, can you just make PB&Js for yourselves? There are some apple slices in the fridge too. Em, pour milk for you and Maddie, please."

Maddie and I made our sandwiches and sat down to eat. Mom had the news on in the kitchen. A news reporter was in Joplin and they showed the mess that was left of their town. You couldn't even tell it was a town. It looked like a junkyard or a garbage dump. The news reporter even looked like she was going to cry as she continued her comments: "The National Weather Service has rated this an EF5 multiple-vortex tornado, over a mile in width. It then tracked eastward across Interstate 44 into parts of Jasper and Newton Counties."

"Hey, we're in Jasper County!" Maddie shouted.

I looked up at Mom. "That same tornado is what came here?" I asked.

Mom answered, "Well, I guess so."

The news program then switched to the weatherman, who jumped right into the forecast: "There is a chance for severe weather again this afternoon, leading into tonight. Heavy rain is expected, along with a chance for damaging winds and a possible tornado."

I got up from the table. "Does Dad know the weather is going to be bad again? He's going to be driving. Where will he go for shelter if there's another tornado?"

Wide eyed, Maddie nodded and asked, "Yeah, will Dad be okay, Mom?"

Putting a hand on our backs, Mom nodded. "Yes, girls. He's used to driving around during the storms to spot funnel clouds, remember? He's been well trained and knows what he's doing. That's why he goes to weather classes all the time—to learn about storm spotting and safety. We just need to pray for all of the people in Joplin and all of the people going there to help."

I wanted to feel better because of what Mom said . . . but all I could think about was another tornado hitting Joplin—or our area.

Chapter 8

It was already raining when Mom took me to play practice after lunch in Dad's car. I felt like my PB&J might come right back up with all the butterflies in my stomach because of going to swim camp and worrying about Dad and wondering if we were going to get another tornado.

We spent the first half of practice on scenes one through three and then broke into groups. One group went with the music director to work on a song, one group stayed with the head director to work on lines, and I got to go with the choreographer and the other kids that would be in the first dance number.

I guess I must have been catching on pretty well because Blake, our choreographer, pointed to me and said, "Emily, will you stand here in the front? The kids can follow you if they get lost."

The dance was awesome. The music had a jumpy beat to it, and we had lots of positions and moves to do in a row. Luckily a lot of parts repeated, but it was still tricky. I jumped up and clapped when I had it all figured out. "Yes! I've got it now!" I whispered to myself.

I was having so much fun, I completely forgot about all of my worries for a while.

We ran through it a few more times, and when we all gathered together again, we got to show Logan, our head director. He loved it. "Emily, the second time the music does that funky part, I want everyone else to freeze and just you do the repeat. Everyone else can join in on the third time."

I felt on top of the world. I almost squealed! *Logan picked me for a special part! I have a solo. Yes!*

I was on cloud nine until practice was over—and then I saw the real clouds outside. They had that scary green tinge to them again. Back in the car, Mom didn't disagree when I said, "The sky looks a lot like a couple days ago."

"I know. Let's hope for just rain and thunder this time."

When we got home, the house smelled like garlic bread. *Mmmmm . . . spaghetti.* That made me feel warm inside.

Maddie and I set the table, and we ate our spaghetti while watching news coverage of Joplin.

"Do you think Dad's there yet?" I asked.

Mom shook her head. "He said it would take about nine hours to get there, so probably not yet."

"Do you think he'll be on the news?" Maddie asked.

I rolled my eyes. I was just about to say, "I doubt it," when I heard the tornado siren start sounding. My whole body tensed as I dropped my fork and looked at Mom. She looked as surprised as we were.

"What on earth?" Mom said. She got up and looked out the window. "It's not bad out yet. Just some rain. It's not even windy."

She spoke too soon. I'd just started glancing around for the cats when the hail started pelting the roof and windows. Mom turned on the police scanner. A moment later Grandma called and said it was really bad out by her house and that we should take cover. Mom grabbed Lucy, and Maddie and I each held a cat. We headed into the master bedroom and found that Dad had left the lid to the crawl space pried open before he left. We sat down on the floor just outside the closet, each holding an animal. The police scanner soon reported that someone had spotted a funnel cloud and possible touchdown out by the college.

"Grandma lives out that way!" I cried.

Maddie surprised me by putting some thought into what was going on: "What if this tornado's already been where Dad is traveling?"

Mom held Lucy close to her. "We're going to stay right here unless we start to hear the freight train noise that everyone says tornadoes sound like. If we hear it, we jump down into the crawl space with the animals. Got it?"

Maddie and I both nodded.

"Can't we go down now?" Maddie said, her voice just above a whisper.

Mom looked at me and then Maddie. "No, not yet. If we go in now, I'm afraid the cats will take off in the crawl space and it will be hard to find them or get them back up into the house when it's over. Let's pray, okay, girls?"

"Okay," Maddie said.

I just nodded and closed my eyes, then swallowed hard.

"Lord," Mom said, "please protect Dad as he travels to help those already affected. Please have the devastation in Joplin draw those who are hurting closer to you. Lord, please protect Grandma and her home as well as the whole town of Rensselaer. We know you have a perfect plan, and there is a reason for everything you do and allow. We know you teach us not to be afraid, so please help us to be brave and have faith in your will. Lord, thank you for all you do for us and for all of our many blessings. Help Matt and the team of guys to be a blessing to others as well. We love you, Lord, amen."

Maddie and I both said, "Amen," but I felt even worse.

We sat there for what seemed like forever, listening to the howling wind and updates on the police scanner. We never did end up having to go down into the crawl space. And the power never even went out through the whole thing. We heard that there were some trees down at the college, but the only other damage was to the "Welcome to Rensselaer" sign on that side of town. Grandma had some branches and sticks in her yard, but everyone in her neighborhood was okay. Mom called Dad and told him what happened. He said it had rained, but they were all just fine.

Thank you, God!

Rensselaer still made the morning news the next day. The reporter showed St. Joseph's College and a humongous tree that was completely uprooted, lying on its side. The reporter was standing by the roots. He could have had another person on his shoulders and they wouldn't have reached the top of what was pulled out of the ground!

I could only stare at the tree with wide eyes, saying in my heart again, *Thank you, God, for keeping us safe!*

Chapter 9

Thankfully the rest of the week was pretty uneventful. Swim practice, eat, play practice, eat, talk to Dad on the phone, go to bed. Dad said it was awful in Joplin. After his first full day there, he told us all on speakerphone, "Cows got picked up and thrown way outside their fences. Houses are smashed to piles of wood and bricks. Cars and trucks were hurled like toys and dropped on top of each other. There are things stuck up in trees that heavy machinery will have to come in and get down. The worst thing, though, is a lot of people died or got hurt. I helped direct traffic and did some recovery work, but we haven't found anyone. I just had no idea how bad it could be. It's heartbreaking."

By Saturday the weather in our area was much better. We went out to help Grandma pick up sticks in the morning and she made us lunch. Then we drove out to see my other grandparents—on the opposite side of town. We visited for a bit, then rode paddleboats on their pond. We saw a big turtle in the cattails; I tried to catch it with Grandpa's fishing net but couldn't.

Mom said it was too big to put in a tank to keep as a pet anyway.

I told Grandpa, "If you ever see a baby one, catch it for me. I've always wanted a turtle."

He smiled. "I've never seen a baby turtle in all the years we have lived out here, but I'll let you know."

Mom gave us a look. "I think we have enough pets at our house."

I frowned and rolled my eyes.

Before long, Mom said, "We need to head home. Let's get ready to go, girls."

Once we got back, I felt too tired to even get a shower, but I still double-checked everything before bed, especially since Dad was gone. When my head finally hit my pillow, I fell right to sleep and slept hard—beat from our first full week of summer break.

On Sunday at church, the pastor said a special prayer for Dad and the others who went to Joplin to help. After the prayer the pastor announced that the group had checked in that morning and said they would be coming home in a few days.

I looked up and smiled. *Thank you, God!*

And the good news kept getting better. We celebrated Memorial Day on Monday with a cookout at our house. Grandma came over, as well as my cousins. Then, when we woke up on Tuesday, Mom said we weren't going to swim practice because we had dentist appointments. I normally didn't like going to the dentist, but it got me out of swim practice and I also knew it could very well be the day I finally got my braces off. The orthodontist at the dentist's office kept telling me I was getting closer and closer. She even said at my last appointment that this appointment could be *the* day. Maddie wasn't a big fan of the dentist either. She didn't even have braces yet, but I guessed her day would come. She'd had a cavity before, so she was always worried she'd get another one and have to get it filled. She also couldn't stand the fluoride treatments.

The hygienist called us back, and we went into two separate rooms to get our teeth cleaned. Mom normally went with Maddie—I figured because she was younger—but today she walked back with me.

"I have a feeling today's the day, Emily," Mom whispered. "You may have a new smile soon!"

Sure hope she's right.

The hygienist cleaned my teeth and then let Dr. Sy know that I was ready for her.

When Dr. Sy came in and looked at my mouth, she smiled. "Are you ready to get these things off, Emily? I think they've done what they needed to do."

I laughed and smiled. "Yes! I'm more than ready."

It took awhile to get everything off, and once it was all over, it felt really weird to run my tongue along my teeth. They handed me a mirror and I smiled into it. *Much better! One less object on my face.*

"Mom," I said. "Can we go to the movies later so I can eat popcorn and licorice and Milk Duds? I haven't had them for two years!"

Mom laughed. A hygienist came in just as she was about to answer. "Maddie's all done. Is it okay if she hangs out here with you, or do you want her out in the waiting room?"

Before Mom could reply, Maddie came trudging into the room with a disgusted look on her face.

"What's wrong, Maddie?" Mom asked. "Did you have a cavity?"

"No! The fluoride treatment tasted awful! They said it was bubble gum flavored, but the only way that could be true is if it was bubble gum that someone scraped off the bottom of a shoe after they stepped in dog poop!"

Mom laughed. "Where do you come up with this stuff?"

Maddie just stared at me. "Hey, you got your braces off!"

I nodded and gave a big smile.

Then Mom said, "Maddie, do you want to go to the movies tonight? Emily's eager to eat all of the foods that were forbidden while she had her braces."

"Sure!"

On our way out, Mom set up our appointments for next time. "Now we just need to get our eye therapy appointments scheduled and we'll be all caught up!"

Maddie and I both groaned at the same time. We had to go to eye therapy for our vision issues since we both had varying degrees of strabismus. They had us do a bunch of eye muscle exercises to train our brains to work with both eyes at the same time. Maddie had to go to therapy every other week, but I'd graduated to only going once a month.

After play practice that day, Maddie and Mom picked me up and we had hard-shell tacos and corn on the cob for dinner. I hadn't had sweet, buttery corn on the cob in two years! It was so good. My face was a mess, but I didn't care. I cleaned myself up, and then we drove to the theater to see *Kung Fu Panda 2*. I of course had popcorn and Milk Duds. By the time the movie was over, I felt like I was going to barf—maybe a little too much of a good thing.

When we got home, I FaceTimed each of my cousins and then Hailey and Lauren to show them my new smile. Then Mom, Maddie, and I all talked to Dad, who said they would be home soon enough. After that I brushed and flossed my straight teeth and did my checks on everything in the house. I hopped into bed, ran my tongue across my teeth one more time, and closed my eyes, feeling a lot better than I had in a while—even though I still didn't like the thought of going to swim camp next week. That was one dark cloud that wouldn't go away.

Chapter 10

I woke up the next morning thinking I heard Dad's voice in the kitchen. I hopped out of bed and ran in to see if it was him.

"Dad!" I shouted.

He came toward me and gave me a big hug, looking almost like he'd cry again. "Oh, I love you, Em. I missed you—all of you."

"Love you too, Dad."

He smiled at me. "Let's go get Maddie up."

We crept into Maddie's room, and Dad put his hand on her back. She groaned and then opened an eye.

"Dad, you're home!" She popped up and reached her hands around Dad's neck. "When did you get home?"

"I drove through the night. The last place I searched for survivors late yesterday had a bunch of girls' toys scattered throughout the debris. It made me keep thinking of you two, and after we talked on the phone, I just had to come home. I told the others I needed to leave, and they were all fine with it." He looked from me to Maddie. "I just wanted to be here with you."

Mom made pancakes with fresh blueberries from the farmer's market. They tasted so sweet and buttery, we didn't even really need syrup.

When we finished eating, Dad looked at the calendar on the fridge. "Emily, there's another storm class tonight. Why don't you go with me? You can learn all kinds of things about the clouds and what to look for during a storm."

"Uh . . . okay, sure. I'll go."

Might be interesting. At least I'll learn when to take cover.

Since Dad wasn't going to work that day, he took us to swim practice. I'm sure after he dropped us off, he drove home and slept like a log—one of those deep sleeps when his snores were long and loud and practically shook the walls.

Later that same day my neighbor, Liza, needed a ride to play practice. Mom and her mom worked out a schedule so that we could take turns carpooling for the rest of the practices. Liza was a year younger than me, and this was her first year in the play. We were both in the dance numbers together. I had always liked Liza. She was easy to talk to and smiled a lot.

"Emily," she said after practice ended, "I'm so glad you're in front of me during that long song. If I get lost or forget the next part, I just look at you!"

That night, Dad and I went to storm class together. I was the only kid there, surrounded by a bunch of men and women from the city and county police departments.

"Are you sure I'm supposed to be here?" I asked Dad.

"Yep, it's open to the public. This guy loves to teach, and he knows what he's talking about because he's a meteorologist."

That didn't mean much to me, because Dad usually joked about the weather guy on TV: "That must be the easiest career in the world. It's the only job you can be wrong most of the time and not get fired!"

Dad and I both took notes, and the teacher handed out pictures of clouds. I learned about the way they rate tornadoes, how to spot clouds or conditions that might create one, and how to be safe if a tornado touched down.

As class went on, I thought maybe I could go to school to be a meteorologist. Then again, I didn't think they would let me skip work on the days that tornadoes were possible. I would need to report on what was happening no matter what. *Maybe not the job for me . . .*

I'm still glad I went to the class, though. I felt a tiny bit better about tornadoes. When we got home, I told Maddie all the stuff I learned.

She didn't care. "When I hear that tornado siren, I'm jumping in the crawl space. That's all I need to know!" Maddie got up from the couch and asked Mom, "What bag should I bring to swim camp? I want to start packing."

Mom laughed, "You've got plenty of time to get ready!"

Maddie insisted, "I'm just excited and want to make sure I have everything I need."

As I watched the two of them head to Maddie's room, I frowned. It felt like a tornado was forming in my stomach. In less than a week we would be heading to swim camp.

Chapter 11

Maddie was so annoying the day we left for swim camp at Purdue. She kept talking about the underwater camera, and meeting an Olympic diver who would be speaking, and getting to swim every day.

I had plenty of my own thoughts. What if we couldn't find our way from the dorm building to the pool—or to the cafeteria for the meals each day? What if we got lost on that big campus? We wouldn't know anyone. I didn't even know if the dorm rooms had locks on the doors. I'd even heard you had to leave your room to go to the bathroom down the hall. What if I had to pee in the middle of the night? I was NOT going out in the hallway in the dark to the restroom! Someone could be hiding somewhere along the way, or in the restroom. There were stories on the news all the time about bad things happening to college students. If college kids couldn't keep bad things from happening, how were an eight- and eleven-year-old supposed to protect themselves?

On the way to Purdue, Maddie fell asleep. I just clenched my teeth and wiped away a few more tears from my eyes. How in the world could she possibly be calm enough to sleep? I was clinging to Brownie, curled up in my seat next to Maddie. With as much crying as I had been doing, my eyes would look like giant puffballs.

Mom and Dad knew I was upset, of course, since I'd been crying pretty much since I'd gotten out of bed.

Now, with Maddie asleep and me unable to stop crying, Mom turned in her seat and said, "Honey, you're going to be just fine. Remember . . . you're the big sister. You need to be brave for Maddie so you don't get her all freaked out too. We wouldn't send you off to something we felt was dangerous. And it's going to be a great time, you'll see. You just need to relax and learn from the coaches and have fun. You and Maddie can order pizza tonight if you want. We can get you a shirt or something from the bookstore when we come to pick you up Saturday too."

When Dad got off at the Purdue exit, I started feeling hot. I tried pointing the vent toward me more, but I couldn't get enough air.

"Can you turn up the air back here?" I asked.

Then it seemed like the van started getting dark. I called out for Mom. And then I started breathing really fast.

"I can't do this!" I shouted. "I'm gonna be sick!"

They can't say I didn't warn them. Poor Brownie got the worst of it. Dad swerved over to the side of the road, yelling something or other. I just remember my stomach lurching and feeling all sweaty. Maddie woke up, and everyone was flinging doors open and flapping around like chickens. If I wouldn't have been so upset, I would've enjoyed watching them all deal with the payment for their cruelty.

After cleaning up the van the best we could, everyone got back in and then started complaining about the smell. I just cried some more. This had to be one of the worst days of my life. I could not understand how Maddie felt so differently. Maybe she was too young to understand all of the dangers out there. Everyone was always saying, "Maddie's carefree." Well, she was definitely carefree about her bedroom—it was always a mess.

When we pulled into the designated parking lot at Purdue, we unloaded our things and walked into the building with the "Welcome Swimmers!" banner. Maddie didn't even pay attention to any of the instructions they were giving us about meals and practices and lights-out. She just figured I would take care of everything, I guess. Then we were released to find our dorm rooms and say goodbye to our parents. We got to the room, and Mom gave me some medicine for my headache.

Maddie threw her stuffed elephant, Sprinkles, on the bed she wanted. "I get top bunk!" she said.

That's when it hit me that Brownie was puke-drenched, squished into a plastic grocery bag in the van. I wouldn't even have *him* to help me cry myself to sleep. I lost it. Again.

Just then an announcement came over the hallway overhead speakers, stating that we needed to say our goodbyes and change into our suits for orientation and some fun time in the pool.

My heart raced. I had nothing to lose. I grabbed onto Mom and begged, "Please! Take me home! Don't make me stay!"

Before Mom could say anything, one of the camp coaches popped in through the open door. I didn't even care that she saw me crying. I didn't care about anything except going home.

"Hi everyone! I'm Coach Melissa." She looked at Maddie and then me. "You need to get your suits on and come with me, girls." She turned and headed out into the hall. "And don't forget your towels! We're meeting at the end of the hall in five minutes." With that she closed the door.

"See, Emmy," Mom said, "they're going to be with you and get you where you need to go for everything during the camp. We're going now. If you need anything, they said you can talk to the camp counselor about using the phone."

Mom and Dad gave each of us hugs, then Dad said a quick prayer for us.

Finally, they headed for the door, where Mom turned and said, "We love you, girls. Have fun."

"Love you!" Maddie shouted.

"Love you," I forced through tears.

It was one of those times you don't feel very loved or loving, but you don't want to regret not saying it if something should happen.

They shut the door behind them, and Maddie moved like lightning. She got her suit on and stuffed a towel under her arm.

"Let's go, Em! I want to swim in the big pool. Did you see all the diving boards in the picture? I wonder which ones we're allowed to go off of?"

I pulled the suit out of my bag and sat on the edge of the bed. Maddie was driving me nuts with all her talk.

"Let's go, Em, c'mon! Now we only have three minutes!"

I started thinking about the diving boards. What if they made us go off them? Some of them were up really high, like as high as our house, or at least our garage. I heard the top one was ten meters high. *Over thirty feet high!* A belly flop off of that could kill you. Even if you were lucky enough to end up feet first, you'd be hurling down so fast from that height, you'd be pummeled deep into the water. And I thought I heard the pool was almost twenty feet deep. You could run out of breath before you reached the surface again. I was NOT going off their diving boards, and I decided that I had to keep Maddie off of them too. Her little carefree self would probably jump off any of them if they let her.

Once I had my suit on, we headed out to the end of the hall. Coach Melissa led us out the doors to the aquatic center. You could smell the chlorine before she even opened the doors. Looking around, I saw more than one pool—and lots of diving boards in the diving well. Tons of kids were there, and everyone seemed excited to get in the water except me. I was probably the only one forced to go there to babysit her little sister.

As the coaches talked to all of us about what we'd be doing over the next three days, I started feeling a little dizzy. I whispered to Maddie, "I need to sit down." But she wasn't paying attention, as usual. I started to walk up to Melissa, but then things got really dark. I couldn't see or hear anything. Then came the sweat. I felt like I couldn't breathe.

The next thing I knew, I was lying on my back, surrounded by a bunch of coaches and kids, and I had a horrible headache.

I saw Maddie kneeling next to me. She had tears rolling down her cheek and she was trying to hold my hand, but Melissa said, "You're going to have to move back, honey."

Then I saw a couple of EMTs, who asked me questions.

"What's your name, sweetie? Are you hurting anywhere?"

I pointed to my head. "My head hurts."

"Ok, just lie still. Can you tell me your name?"

I could feel my heart racing, but I felt safe with the EMTs there. After they checked me over completely, they put me on one of those big stretcher boards and carried me to some kind of trainer's room in the building, with Coach Melissa following. I saw her hold a hand out to block Maddie.

"You'll have to stay put, hon. We'll take care of her."

Once in the room they sat me up, and I saw blood on one of the white towels Melissa was holding. I realized that was probably why the back of my head was throbbing. It hurt worse the more I thought about it. I started feeling woozy all over again.

As the EMTs worked on bandaging up my head, Melissa looked down at me and said, "We called your parents and they're coming back right now."

I gave a little nod. Mom and Dad probably hadn't even made it too far down the road yet. I could only imagine how disappointed they would be that their plan to force me to go to swim camp didn't work out and that they wasted their money. They should have realized it when I barfed in the van. They could've let me out of it then. But, nope, it had to take a bloody, cracked head to teach them how dangerous this was.

At least I was going home.

Then I saw Maddie peeking in through one of the room's windows. Her friend Kennedy was standing next to her. I frowned. What was Maddie going to do? She wouldn't have a roommate, and she wasn't allowed to room alone because of her age. Maddie was actually one of the youngest swimmers there.

She'll be so upset if she has to leave because of me.

When Mom and Dad got there a few minutes later, I thought they were going to yell at me, but they were actually pretty worried about my head. They talked to the EMTs, and we were all happy to hear that I didn't have to go to the hospital. Now Mom and Dad had to decide if they were going to let Maddie stay or not. Melissa said that they could put her in a room with two other girls if she wanted to. That's when Kennedy volunteered their room, and Mom and Dad both said it would be fine. Maddie was thrilled. She came up and gave all of us a hug.

Then she grabbed my hand. "I was praying for you when they carried you in here."

I had to admit that Maddie could be really sweet sometimes. And I was happy she got to stay.

We said our goodbyes to Maddie, then Dad took me out to the van while Mom went to the dorm room to get my stuff.

As we left campus, Mom apologized for forcing me to come—kind of. "Emily, I'm sorry that you got yourself so worked up that you got physically sick. We'll have to find a way for you to work on this fear of yours. I'm going to talk to Pastor Joe and set up an appointment for us to help you through this."

I just nodded and thought about what Mom said. Pastor Joe—better known as "PJ"—was really nice. He always made every person in the church feel like they were his favorite person. He reminded me of the vet we took Lucy to. Dr. Mallory also acted like your dog was the most special animal in the whole world.

PJ liked to give everyone a hug, whether they were a kid or a grandpa. Sometimes he would give you a piece of candy too.

As I stared out the window, I decided that talking to PJ would be way better than having to learn to face my fears by being forced to stay somewhere. Maybe there was hope.

Maybe . . .

Chapter 12

On Saturday afternoon Maddie came home from swim camp with Dad, all excited to show us her video from the underwater camera. I had to admit, it was pretty cool.

"I got to go off of the diving board, but only the low one. Flip-turns are really easy for me now too!"

I could tell how proud she felt. She and Kennedy definitely seemed to have a great time. I was really glad that she got to stay—and even gladder that I got to leave.

Luckily, swimming would be over for me in one more week. Some swimmers would swim a whole extra week after that if they were invited to compete in the conference meet. Only the top two swimmers in each event got to go. Maddie would be swimming for her age group at the conference in four events.

I had other things to look forward to. I would have my first appointment with PJ on Monday, and I still had the chance to work on the play for a couple more weeks and then perform in it. I couldn't wait to get up on stage and show everyone our dances and costumes.

Maddie must not have gotten much sleep at swim camp because she fell asleep on the couch right after dinner. Dad had to carry her to bed. Mom patted the spot next to her on the love seat and smiled at me. I sat down next to her.

"When you meet with PJ, you can ask him anything or tell him anything. We all just want to help you get over your fears of tornadoes and fires, staying over at friends' houses, and worrying something bad is going to happen all the time."

Dad came back into the room just as Mom finished talking. "Yes, honey. We don't want you to be stressed out over everything. You have plenty of time for that when you get older."

Mom shot Dad a look. "Nice. That's reassuring."

Dad laughed. "Really, Emily. You're at the age that it's good to learn what you like and don't like. If you don't try out new things, you won't know. You'll just assume you don't like any of it."

Mom put her arm around me. "We want you to make good memories and not live in fear. Life is too short to worry all the time."

Life can be even shorter if you aren't careful. I got up and gave Mom and Dad a hug, then said good night and went to my room to get ready for bed. As I waited for them to go to their room, I thought about my meeting with PJ on Monday. I sure hoped he had a way to help me not be such a chicken. *Maybe tonight I won't double-check the locks.*

I lay there and listened as Mom and Dad shut off the TV. I heard the faucet running while they brushed their teeth. I heard the TV in their bedroom turn on and their door click shut. I just lay there. It was so comfy in my bed. I really didn't want to get up to check the doors. *I may be able to fall asleep without doing it.*

Lucy was already asleep by my side. I tried praying: "God, can you please make sure those doors are locked and protect our house tonight? Can you help me sleep without going out there to check them? Can you give PJ advice for me on Monday that will help me stay at friends' houses? Can you keep the tornadoes and fires away from our house? And all of my family's houses? Oh, and my friends' houses? Well, I don't want any tornadoes or fires for anyone. I guess I'm asking a lot. Let's just start with tonight. Will you protect everyone tonight? Thank you, God, amen."

I thought about how many other people probably pray for these things and how sometimes bad things would happen anyway. *Why do some people have to have tornadoes and fires and break-ins? I'm sure some of those people prayed to not have that happen.*

Then I heard a crash out in the kitchen. I shot out of bed like a flash and ran out to see what was going on. In the sink I saw a broken glass and milk splattered all over the counter. Dad walked out to see what was going on too. Then I noticed a bunch of papers scattered on the floor, but no one was in sight. I swallowed and took a deep breath.

Dad surveyed the crime scene, then said, "Looks like Maddie left her milk out on the counter from dinner and the cats tried to get it."

A second later Mom peeked her head out from the hallway. "Everything okay?"

I nodded. "Yeah, the cats knocked Maddie's milk glass into the sink." I leaned down and started picking up the papers from the floor. "I think they tore out of here across all of my 4-H papers, because the cats are nowhere in sight and I know I didn't leave my stuff all over the floor!"

Mom laughed, said good night, then headed back to bed.

I watched as Dad picked up the glass pieces, wiped up the milk, and then headed out of the kitchen.

"Good night, Em."

"Night."

Since I was up, I went ahead and checked both doors before I went back to my room. I was up anyway. Maybe the whole cat thing was God's way of getting me up to check them.

Chapter 13

On the way to swim practice Monday morning, Mom ran through our schedules. "Emily, you're going to church to see PJ after lunch and then right to play practice. Maddie, after I drop Em off at play practice, you have an eye therapy appointment."

Maddie groaned. "How much longer until I get to just go once a month, like Emmy?"

"Maybe next year, hon. You'll be glad you did this when you're older. You don't want to wear bifocals your whole childhood or have a crossed eye when you're older.

"When do I have to go next, Mom?" I asked.

"Not until the end of summer."

"Good." I smiled.

Maddie shot me the stink-eye.

I scarfed down my lunch that day, eager to go talk to PJ. He never seemed afraid of anything. Maybe he would teach me the right way to pray.

When we got to the church, Mom led me to PJ's office. He walked right over to me and gave me a giant hug. His wife, Sara, was there too. I loved Sara. She was my youth group leader.

Then he hugged Mom and said, "You can stay in here or wait out in the hall or run an errand and come back. Whatever you want to do."

Mom stepped toward the door. "I'll just wait out here. I can check my emails on my phone and hang out until you all are done." She closed the door.

PJ sat at his desk and motioned for me to sit in the chair by Sara. "How's your summer going, Em?"

"Fine, except for swimming. It's not my favorite."

"Are you in the play again this year?"

"Yep, I have practice right after we're done here."

"Well, Sara and I will have to come to the play and see you. Make sure you let us know about tickets."

I smiled. "Okay, sure."

An awkward silence followed—at least it felt awkward to me.

Then PJ got down to business. "So, your mom said you have a hard time when there are storms. Can you tell us about that?"

This was when I was supposed to tell him what a big chicken I was, and he would tell me what a small chance there was of my house being hit by a tornado. But I just said, "Yeah, I don't like storms, and I worry that a tornado will hit our house."

PJ nodded, as if he knew I was going to say that. "What do you do when you worry?"

I shrugged. "Mostly I get shaky and try to think about what could happen, and sometimes I pray."

"Tornadoes can be really destructive. I'm sure your dad told you about the awful mess Joplin was. Are there other things that scare you or worry you as much as the tornadoes?"

"Um . . . yeah. Fires, robbers, staying over anywhere but my own house, doing anything dangerous . . . any kind of bad stuff that can happen to you."

PJ gave a little smile and nodded again. "It's normal to not want bad stuff to happen to you or your family. It's human to be scared sometimes. God doesn't give us a spirit of fear, though. And think about it: when you worry, does it help you feel better?"

"No. It makes me sick."

"Okay. And when you worry, does it make it less likely that the tornado or fire or robbers will come?"

"Well . . . no, I guess not."

"Who is the only one that can make those things more or less likely to happen?"

"God."

"Yes. God is in control. Not you, Sis. No matter how much you don't want something to happen or how much you worry, you can't control any of it."

I looked down and thought about that, then looked up again. "So how should I pray when I'm afraid?"

"You can thank God for your many blessings. You can ask for his protection and to keep Satan away. God wants you to come to him in praise and to seek him for comfort. All things are done for his glory—even the bad things."

I shook my head. "But why does he let the bad things happen?"

"Everything that happens is part of his perfect plan. Even something as bad as the tornado in Joplin has many blessings and, in some ways, drew people closer to him and to each other. The next time you're afraid, try praying. Remember that whatever happens is part of God's plan. If you still feel scared, you can call us. I don't care what time it is. I always have my cell phone on."

I smiled at him. "Okay, thanks."

PJ prayed for me, then got up and opened the door to tell Mom we were done. He went back to his desk, wrote his phone number on a Post-it note and handed it to me, and gave me a fist bump. Sara gave me a hug.

PJ looked at Mom. "She can call us if she needs to . . . anytime."

Mom waved goodbye to PJ and Sara. "Thanks so much for meeting with her."

He nodded. "Let me know a good time for her to come back next week."

"Goodbye . . . and thanks," I said.

He gave me a thumbs-up, then we left the church and headed to play practice.

I can't say I felt all right about my fears, but maybe it would be a little better now. Maybe with each time we met, I'd get a teeny tiny bit braver.

Chapter 14

Not much happened the next week, except the end of swimming practice for me. Yay! On the last day, our coaches let all the kids who were not going to conference have a fun practice. We played water polo and sharks and minnows. We also got to dive for cans of pop in the diving well. Maddie and all of the other conference swimmers had a regular practice in the pool with lanes. They only had a week left to prepare for the big meet. Bummer for them!

I practically skipped out of practice that day. Mom asked, "What's got you so excited?"

"I'm done with swimming! You said next year I get to choose if I swim or not, so I'm done! Done! Done! Done!"

Mom chuckled. "Well, you'll have to do something to remain active. You can walk Lucy every day, go for a jog in the neighborhood, or ride your bike, or something. You can't just sit around. Exercise is important."

"I know some of the fall sports start conditioning soon. A lot of my friends have been talking about it. Maybe I could try one out."

I could see if I liked jogging and join the cross-country team. Mom loved running. And how hard could it be? A lot of the swimmers were also on the cross-country team.

"Maybe I'll try out for the cross-country team."

You would have thought I just told Mom she won teacher of the year. She got this wild, happy look on her face. "Really, Em? I didn't even know you were thinking about that! I can train you. You can run with me anytime. We can get you some good running shoes and some running shorts and maybe we can even run the Race for Autism 5K next month together! This's going to be great! Oh, honey, I'm so excited you're going to run."

"Whoa! Slow down, Mom. I said *maybe*. I don't like running in PE, but maybe this'll be different. And I'm not running in any 5K races. That's too far. I'm pretty sure the races for cross-country runners my age are less than two miles, and that's all I'm doing."

Mom smiled all night. I think she was even humming when she made dinner. Crazy lady. I didn't even realize the middle school cross-country coach was one of the elementary teachers at Mom's school. Mom of course called him as soon as dinner was over to find out all the details about summer practice. She was giddy.

I tried to run with Mom that week, but she didn't know how to go slow. I could hardly breathe and was sweating the first time we went around the block.

I decided I would just run with the team and not at home. I hoped it would be better with other kids who had short legs like me. If nothing came of this, at least I got some cool running shoes and shorts out of the deal.

Our first practice was awful. It was seventy degrees out and I felt like I was going to pass out. I walked back to the park shelter where we started from and sat down with some water. The next day wasn't much better. The rest of the week only got worse. I was sore from what little running I did do, and I felt sick every time I ran. I got really good at handing out water bottles to everyone else since I quit way before them every time. I told Hailey I didn't think I could do it.

Hailey said it would get better once the actual season started in the fall. "The summer conditioning is the worst part because it's hot and we run more than our normal practices during the season. Practices are way more fun once school starts because there's a scavenger hunt day each week where we have to run to different locations to get our workout in. Meets are fun too. We ride a bus to them and have a meal together afterward. We hang out a lot outside of practice too. It's all worth it. Hang in there."

It sounded like it *could* be fun, but what if I got overheated and passed out? What if I got last place every time? It would feel like being back on the swim team again. What if after all that work . . . my friends still didn't want to hang out with me because they'd moved on to other friends?

Then Hailey asked, "Do you want to come over and spend the night after play practice today?" That was the first time I had been asked since I'd chickened out at the beginning of the summer.

"Let me ask my mom and I'll let you know." I actually kind of wanted to. Of course, I knew Mom would be all for it.

I gulped some more Gatorade, waved goodbye to Hailey, and climbed into the van.

"Mom, Hailey wants to know if I can stay over at her house tonight."

Mom's eyes got all excited. "I've got a good feeling about this time. Just remember what PJ talked to you about and hang in there."

I told myself to be brave. I wanted to be brave. And I was brave—until Hailey fell asleep around midnight. I figured I must be like Cinderella. Everything was fine until the clock struck twelve and then everything fell apart and the fun was over, but just for her.

I tried to read with my flashlight. I tried to go through the entire play in my head to pass the time. I prayed for protection and comfort. I even went to their front and back door to be sure they were locked. I found her smoke detectors and made sure they all flashed to show they had good batteries. I checked the weather forecast on my phone and it looked perfectly fine. There was no good reason I should be afraid. I still just wanted to be in my own bed. I wanted Mom and Dad close by. *What is God's plan in this for me?* I thought for a moment. *God would want me to sleep.* But I was only going to sleep if I was at home.

I nudged Hailey.

"Huh? What? Oh . . . what do you need, Em?"

"I think I better go home."

She yawned. "Are you sick or something?"

"No . . . just homesick."

Hailey got up to get the phone but came back and told me it wasn't on the cradle. So she knocked on her mom and dad's door. "Mom?"

"What do you want, Hailey?" her dad called out.

"Emily wants to go home and needs to call her mom. Where's the phone?"

Hailey's mom got up and came to her room. "C'mon, Emily. I'll take you home. "

As we drove home, I thought about how good it would have felt to wake up at Hailey's and have breakfast at her house. How happy Mom and Dad would have been that I'd made it through the night. They would've probably been beaming when I came home, telling me how brave I was.

When we pulled up to my house, I thanked Mrs. Lewis. "I'm sorry I got you up. Thank you for the ride home and for having me."

"It's okay. Now get in there and get some sleep. You've got to run in about seven hours."

I rang the doorbell. It seemed like forever before Dad answered the door. He wasn't very happy to see me. He didn't even say a word. He waved at Hailey's mom and shut the door behind us. Then he walked to his room. I locked the front door, checked the back door, and went to bed, squeezing Brownie as tight as I could to hold back my frustrated tears.

Chapter 15

The next day at practice a bunch of the runners were talking about going shopping together at the mall to find dresses for the Back-to-School Bash, and then spend the night at one of their houses. It sounded like a lot of fun, aside from the part about spending the night somewhere. I didn't hear all of it because they were running way ahead of me. I figured I would hear the details sometime before the trip was planned.

I was wrong.

That afternoon, after play practice, I saw all kinds of pictures posted of the runners on their shopping trip. There were pictures of them trying on matching outfits, eating ice cream, posing in front of some fountain, and making weird faces. I felt like someone had ripped my heart out and stomped on it. There in the middle of all of them was Hailey. And her mom was the one that took them!

Why didn't she invite me? Was it because I wouldn't stay over afterward? Did they all think I was a baby? Here I was trying to run my butt off to be doing something with them, and I still didn't get to hang out with the group.

Mom walked in on me staring at the computer with tears streaming down my face.

"I saw the pictures Hailey posted," she said. "Are you okay, hon?"

I sniffled and shook my head. "It's all of my friends, Mom. They went without me. I thought Hailey was my friend. I don't see why they didn't ask me. I was just doing cross-country to try to keep my friends, but that obviously isn't working either. I want to quit the team. I hate running."

Mom went from feeling sorry for me to mad. It was kind of like the day I told her I wanted to quit piano—something she loved and wanted to do. Now here I was trying to quit something else she loved. I think she was embarrassed to have the coach, whom she worked with everyday, know that her daughter was a quitter.

"Emily. You're not quitting the team. You have to finish what you started. If you don't want to do it next year, that's fine, but you don't just quit before you've even had your first meet. You don't quit because something's hard, and you don't quit because of some girl drama. Maybe Hailey's mom could only fit so many people in her vehicle, so she had to cut someone and she knew you wouldn't spend the night afterward, so it was you. Not because you aren't Hailey's friend or she doesn't like you. She just tried to have you spend the night last night, but you came home early. She wouldn't have invited you to her house yesterday if she didn't like you. Plus, you had play practice today. You wouldn't have been able to go anyway."

I didn't want to hear any more. She didn't understand. I was stuck doing another sport I hated and with girls who didn't care if I was there or not. I didn't want to go back to cross-country practice on Monday at all.

I begged to not go to the next practice—partly because I would have to face my friends and didn't know what to say to them, and partly because it was going to be hard to run in the heat. All the while I kept thinking about being left out. *What if they didn't ask me because they're mad at me for some reason? What if they just don't like me? What if Hailey told everyone I'm too chicken to spend the night and they all think I'm a baby?*

Mom wouldn't budge, so I had to go to practice on Monday. Hailey came up to me right after I got there. She handed me a headband like the ones she and all the other girls were wearing.

"Hey, got this for you. We're all going to wear these and do the Glow Run together next month. Wanna go? We'll all be in pretty good shape by then and should be able to handle a 5K race. It's at night and you wear glow-in-the-dark stuff, like these headbands. You can register with our group. Search on the form for the Glow Girls and join our team!"

I ran my fingers over the headband, then squeezed it in my hands. I wanted to hug her for thinking of me, even though she didn't ask me to shop with them. Now they were inviting me to do something with them. I could be one of the Glow Girls. There was only one problem: I couldn't run a 5K now and doubted I'd be ready in time for the Glow Run.

Once practice started, I tried really hard to run the whole time and keep up with the other girls. Every time I thought about walking, I sang in my head, *Just put one foot in front of the other*. I tried to push off harder so my stride would take me farther. I tried breathing in through my nose and out through my mouth.

I almost got sick. My side started hurting and I finally had to stop. I walked back to the shelter in tears. I went up to the coach while the others stretched.

"Coach, I'm sure you've figured out by now that I'm not going to help the team win. You may also know that I don't like running. My mom won't let me quit, so I don't know what to do. I know I usually don't give it my all, but today I did. It didn't help."

The coach gave me a little smile. "Emily," he said, "just because your mom loves running doesn't mean you have to. You were brave enough to join the team and give it a shot. I'll tell you what. I would LOVE to have you run on the team, but only if you want to be here. I would even love to have you run on the team if you have to walk half of every race and finish dead last every time. But only if your heart's in it. If you don't like running and don't think you ever will, I'm not going to force you to do it. I think you can think of it as trying, not quitting. You gave it a chance."

I heaved a deep sigh. "Yeah, but my mom won't give me the option to just give it a chance and then quit. She also spent a bunch of money on the shoes and shorts and stuff. She'll be really upset if I give up."

"Okay, then I have an offer for you. What if you became the team manager instead? You would still be an important part of the team, help out at practices, go to all the meets, and that way you wouldn't be quitting the team. What do you think?"

My eyes popped open wide. This guy was a genius! "Yes! That's perfect! I think my mom would even be okay with that. Thanks, Coach."

At the end of practice, I told Hailey about the coach's idea of me being the team manager.

"I'm glad you'll still be on the team," Hailey said. "Will you still try to do the Glow Run with us?"

"Uh . . . I doubt I can run that far."

Hailey didn't give up. "If you need to walk, I'll stay with you and walk as long as you need to. Just think about it. It'll be fun!"

"Okay, thanks! I'll talk to my mom about it. See you tomorrow at practice!"

I couldn't believe she would do that. She was a good runner and could do really well at that race if she gave it her all, but said she would walk with me.

I had come to practice upset about being left out, but now I knew that Hailey cared about me—and that my coach did too.

When Mom picked me up, I told her about managing the team. At first she was disappointed. "You're going to put in all that time going to practices and meets and have nothing to show for it."

I had nothing to say at first, but then I remembered what Mom was always telling me about the importance of service and giving. I said, "Well, I'd be providing a service for the team. Whether I'd be running or not, I still wouldn't have anything to show for it. It's not like I was going to win a bunch of medals or anything. Besides, I can concentrate my efforts on the play, the thing I actually want to do."

She shrugged. "That is true."

"And guess what? Hailey and some other girls on the team are doing the Glow Run next month, and they invited me to be on their team. Hailey said she would walk with me whenever I needed to walk. Can I do it?"

Now Mom smiled. "That's awesome, Em! Yes, how do we get you signed up? That'll be so much fun. I'm glad you're doing it! Does that mean you'll do the Race for Autism 5K with me too?"

"Not unless you're walking most of it!"

Chapter 16

I liked cross-country practice a lot more once I didn't have to worry about running. I got to hang out with Coach while everyone else ran. I got water for them, timed them as they came in, and helped pick up stuff afterward. When Coach ordered T-shirts for the team, he put all of our names on the back, even mine. This managing thing was too good to be true. I got to hang out with everyone, be part of the team, and do NO running! I actually looked forward to the meets.

Play practice, of course, continued to be awesome. Those of us who were dancers basically got to run through our routines the whole time. Another dream come true! I couldn't wait for the actual performance. Liza and I practiced our dances together in the evenings sometimes. She might have been a grade behind me, but it didn't seem like it. Sometimes we got together after dinnertime and would ride bikes or walk the dog together, or just hang out.

Maddie had her conference swim meet and Mom said I didn't have to go, but I went anyway, since Maddie was coming to my play. I also got to see my friends swim that way. I didn't miss swimming a bit. Just the smell of the pool brought back bad memories of swimming and last-place finishes.

I met with PJ and Sara again the next Sunday after church. I thought he would be really disappointed that I'd had the chance to try spending the night again but chickened out. Instead, he just seemed proud that I'd tried again.

"Emily, the important thing is that you did try again. You prayed too. But do you really trust Jesus?"

"Well . . . yeah, of course," I answered.

"Do you understand that he is the one and only being who can make anything happen or not happen? It is in him you need to feel comfort—not your bed, or your house, or with your parents. He is always with you, even when your parents aren't. His grace and love for you should give you hope and peace. Remember to thank him for your blessings and for his plan for you, and remember that he is there—all the time."

I had never thought of it that way. Once a friend would go to sleep, I usually felt creeped out and alone. Now I knew I needed to concentrate on God watching over me. He wouldn't want me to be scared or to try to handle things by myself. *Maybe I can try again before the summer is over . . . if anyone bothers to ask me to stay over again.*

The play performance was in a few days, and our last practices were all dress rehearsals. I loved it when we got to wear our costumes and do our hair. I had a few costume changes for the play; my favorite was a bright yellow dress with an orange sash. Since it was a Dr. Seuss play, some of us had wires in our braids to make it look like our hair was curving upward. We all had different colors sprayed in our hair and we got to wear fun makeup too.

The dress rehearsals were all at night so we could get used to how it would feel on the performance nights. Our director cried at our last practice when we did our curtain call.

"That was fantastic! You all look amazing. You're going to knock their socks off. The first night of the show is sold out already, so tell your parents to get here early if they want a good seat!"

I felt plenty of butterflies when I got up the next morning—not the kind I felt when there was a tornado warning, but the good kind, the kind where you are so excited that you just hope all the way down to your toes that everything goes well.

Chapter 17

People flooded in when the doors finally opened. The auditorium was packed in no time. All of my grandparents and even a couple of my aunts and cousins came to see me in the play. Maddie always insisted on sitting as close to the front as possible so that I could see them from the stage when I looked out. There they all were, clumped in the second row. My family clump. I had disappointed them so many times with swimming, soccer, cross-country, piano, and being scared to stay anywhere. This was my chance to show them what I *could* do. I didn't know why, but I didn't feel afraid on the stage. It just felt good to pretend to be someone else in a made-up world—especially a Dr. Seuss world.

When the music started, I felt all sparkly inside. I couldn't wait for them to pull back that red velvet curtain. Everyone laughed in the right spots and clapped louder than I expected. It was hot up there, but I didn't even mind sweating. I sang louder than I did in practice and danced my butt off. At the very end we did our curtain call, and everyone got up on their feet and clapped some more. When I looked out into the second row, Mom was crying and Dad gave me a thumbs-up high in the air.

We got to come out in our costumes to see our families and have pictures taken. I felt like a star. I couldn't imagine any win at a swim meet feeling like this. It felt like the days back when I got to do my dance recitals. We would come down from the stage with our fancy outfits on, and everyone smiled and said nice things. No one won or lost. They just enjoyed seeing you do what you loved.

Mom handed me a bouquet of flowers and gave me a big hug. She took pictures of me with my cousins and Maddie.

"You did such a great job, Em," she said. "We're so proud of you."

My little cousins looked up at me like I was famous. It was cute.

Then PJ and Sara walked up and hugged all of us. "You did an amazing job, girl! Now I just want to know . . . how'd you get your braids to stick up like that?"

We all laughed. I thanked everyone for coming and went backstage to change.

The next night's performance was even better than the first. We all felt more comfortable and relaxed since we had already done it for a live audience. Mom, Dad, and Maddie came again. Some people from church and a couple of my former teachers came up to me afterward to say I did a good job.

Then I felt a tap on my shoulder. I turned to see Hailey and Lauren smiling at me.

"You did an awesome job, Emily!" Hailey said, reaching out for a high five.

"Thanks for coming, guys! Mom, can you take a picture of us?"

Just then the crowd started heading out and the director, Logan, motioned for us to wrap up our thank-yous and goodbyes so we could start the cast party down the hall.

Mom snapped a quick picture of Hailey, Lauren, and me, and then gave me another hug. "I'll be back to get you at ten," Mom said. "Have fun!"

Then it was off to the cast party! The director's mom was a professional wedding decorator, so the decorations were awesome. Everything looked like it was straight out of a Dr. Seuss book. Logan gave out some funny awards to different cast members, and we ate cookies that looked like green eggs and ham. At the end, when Logan thanked us for our hard work, all of the adults that helped out with the play pulled cans of silly string from behind their backs and came running after us.

Mom was waiting in the hall when it was over. "What was all the screaming?"

"We got attacked with silly string! It was so much fun. I can't wait to do the play again next year." It was one of the best nights ever.

I slept all the way until I had to get up for church the next morning. I woke up happy about the play performances, but also felt sad because it was all over. At church, several people who had seen the play came up to talk to me. I wished I didn't have to wait another whole year before the next play, or at least that I could be in dance classes again.

When we got back in the van after the service, Dad asked, "Where would the big star like to eat lunch?"

I didn't even have to think about it: "Dairy Queen, please!"

It was so nice out that we ate on the patio seating area. I had chicken strips, onion rings, and an Oreo Blizzard. Mmm! My summer was wrapping up great. Only a couple weeks until school started. I was looking forward to managing the cross-country team, walking/running the Glow Run with my friends, and going to the Back-to-School Bash dance. Everything in life was awesome.

Until we got home, and the doorbell rang.

Nothing could have prepared me for the news about to be shared by our visitors.

Chapter 18

I headed into my bedroom to get changed out of my church clothes. The doorbell rang, and Mom went to answer it. It wasn't long before I heard a tap on my door and Mom asked me to come out to the living room. It was PJ and Sara who had dropped by. At least I thought they had just dropped by. I said hi, hugged them, and then turned to go back to my room when Mom asked me to stay and sit down with them. Then I knew this was a planned visit. Maybe they were checking on my progress or meeting with me here instead of at church?

Dad kept taking a breath like he had something to say, but instead he continued making a weird face and looking around. I imagined this was how he looked when he had to explain to a child that he had to lock up her parents because of some bad thing they did.

When he finally spoke, everyone got really quiet. And then my worst nightmare started unfolding. "Emily, we asked PJ and Sara to come over to help us talk to you about something. You know the summer camp that kids from our church go to up at Gull Lake?"

I pulled the pillow from behind me and crunched myself up into a ball on the love seat that I was sharing with Mom. I put the pillow in front of me and scooted farther into the corner away from her.

This can't be happening.

Dad went on, "We signed you up to go this year. It isn't for another week, but we wanted you to know ahead of time to be able to prepare yourself. The play is over now, so you won't miss anything. I'm sure your cross-country coach will be okay with you missing a week of practice, since you are just managing now."

I squeezed back the tears in my eyes and steadied myself before I finally spoke. "I have to go to camp . . . for a week? You signed me up without asking me?"

PJ finally spoke, "Come over here, Sis." He motioned to a spot between him and Sara. I just wanted to run to my room and shut the door. This wasn't fair. Now PJ and Sara would see me crying and know what a scaredy-cat I was. Why couldn't my parents just let me outgrow my fear? Why did I have to fix it right then?

I didn't budge from my spot, so PJ switched seats with Mom. He told me all of this stuff about how fun camp would be and about the times his family had gone. "Emily," he said, "you have to trust that your parents are doing what they feel is the path God would want you on. This camp is a chance for you to learn a lot about yourself and strengthen your faith."

Mom chimed in, "Honey, we know you're afraid to stay overnight at strange places, but you'll be surrounded by loving, Christian people. They'll have counselors there and several people from our church that you know too. If you get scared and cry or need someone to talk you through your fears, it's a safe place to fall apart. No one's going to judge you there. By the end of the week, it'll be no big deal to stay there anymore."

I felt some hot tears and I sniffled as I crushed the pillow in a tighter hug. "Why?" I mumbled. "Why did you do this? At the beginning of summer I couldn't even make it one day at swim camp."

PJ reached out and patted my shoulder. "There are all kinds of things to do at camp. There's a lake with a huge floating trampoline, there's a zip line, a giant swing . . . all kinds of fun stuff. And there are different themed dinner nights, where you dress up different ways. Oh, and there's a talent show one night. Your friend Liza will be there too. You'll have a lot of fun."

I tried to hide my face in the pillow. By listing all of those things PJ had only made everything worse. I could have given them a whole list of reasons why each of those things was a terrible idea for me.

A thought hit me and I looked up. "Is Maddie going?"

Mom and Dad both shook their heads, and PJ said, "No, your parents said she got to go to swim camp, so this one is just for you. Now . . . I have something I want you to do. Read 2 Timothy 1:7: 'For God hath not given us the spirit of fear; but of power, and of love, and of a sound mind.' When you get it memorized, you call me and Sara, and we will take you for an ice cream. We're going to go now. Just remember that you need to trust your parents and God on this one. We'll talk to you soon."

PJ and Sara each gave me a big hug, then left. I ran to my room and locked the door. Surprisingly, Mom and Dad didn't come in for at least an hour. When they finally did, they tried to talk to me about how hard this decision had been for them and how great this was going to be for me.

I couldn't even look at them.

Chapter 19

I had the Timothy verse memorized right away. I knew I wasn't supposed to be scared, but what if I was? It said God has not given us a spirit of fear. How could I get rid of it, then? It also said I'd been given a sound mind and the power of love. I didn't see how that would help me. Maybe PJ could explain what the verse meant. I called him and he said we would meet up and have ice cream together soon.

Mom and Dad were extra nice to me the next several days. I basically went to cross-country practice, came home, ate lunch, and then went to my room until bedtime each night. Then I would cry myself to sleep. I knew my parents loved me, but I didn't know if they *liked* me. Why couldn't they just accept the way I was? They tried to force everything. I didn't like spending the night at other places. I didn't like piano. I didn't like swimming. I didn't like running. I didn't like camps.

I *did* like dancing though. I LOVED it. I wished they could figure out a way for me to take dance lessons the way they figured out ways to make me do the other stuff. But I knew that wasn't going to happen because it wasn't convenient for them. It just wasn't fair. My dad wouldn't like to take dance lessons—I wouldn't try to force him to take dance just because I liked it. I wouldn't like him less because he didn't like to dance. They didn't ever look at it that way, though.

Thursday came. The next day I was supposed to leave for camp. Mom came into my room to help me pack.

"Don't you want to take some things for the themed nights?" she asked. "I have the list here. You could do the Olympics night—just wear your US-flag shirt. The safari night would be fun. Wear your dad's binoculars around your neck and his camo hat. For the—"

"Mom!" I interrupted. "I'm not dressing up for any of the themes."

"Are you going to do something for the talent show?"

"No."

"You could play a song on the piano or read a poem or something."

"No. I don't want to dress up, or do the talent show, or go to camp."

Mom tossed some things in my bag and then left my room. Normally she would push a little harder to get me to do what everyone else was doing, but I think she knew she had already gone too far in making me go to camp.

I sat there thinking about camp. We would be staying in cabins. What if they didn't have locks on them? And I didn't know who was going to be staying in my cabin with me. What if there were people I didn't know? I hoped it would be dark enough in there that no one could see me cry myself to sleep every night . . . if I slept at all. I hoped it was light enough so I could see if anyone was sneaking into our cabin or if there were any bats. What if I didn't like the food there? What if the mosquitoes were horrible? I always swelled up when I got bitten. What if they made me get in the lake? There were fish swimming in there and who knew what else. I was sure people peed in there too.

After lunch PJ and Sara came over and picked me up for ice cream. He told me everything was going to be okay and that he and Sara were praying for me. He also told me about things his kids used to do at camp and how much they missed it now that they were too old to go. *Hmph.* I knew I wouldn't miss it. I couldn't wait to be old enough to not be forced to go to things that I didn't want to go to. How could he say everything would be okay? Bad things happened to people all the time. He couldn't guarantee anything.

That afternoon Liza called and asked if I would do the dance from the play with her for the camp talent show. "We could wear our hair in braids like we did in the play and just wear matching-colored clothes. We already know the dance and my dad said I could buy the song to put on my iPod for them to play for us at the talent show."

What was I supposed to say? She already had everything figured out. What excuse was left to give?

"Uh . . . sure. What color shirts do you want to wear? We could both wear black shorts." I couldn't believe I was agreeing to do the talent show.

When I told Mom about the talent show, you would have thought I told her I was going to run her next race with her. I think she actually had tears in her eyes.

"Oh, Emily, I'm so glad to hear you say that. You're going to be great! You and Liza will have so much fun. Do you want to have her over to practice this evening?"

I shook my head. "No, we just performed it at the play and we know it by heart. I just want to go to my room." I sat in my room on my hot pink foldout chair and stared at my bags.

The verse from 2 Timothy came to mind: *"For God hath not given us the spirit of fear; but of power, and of love, and of a sound mind."*

I sighed, then whispered, "God, I need your help with this one. I know it's church camp, and you probably want me to go too. Please help me to not be scared and take care of me while I'm there. Or better yet, please give me the wisdom to figure out a good way to get out of it. You can make me sick . . . or some emergency could happen that wouldn't hurt anyone—just cause the camp to be closed or something. A water main break would be good because the water would not be safe to use for a couple days. Maybe a bear could come, and camp would need to be closed until they could capture it and relocate it. Or maybe a film director will need to use the camp this week to shoot a scene for a movie, and we would have to stay off the set. There are a lot of things you could make happen that would get me out of this without costing money or pain."

A few minutes later, Mom came in to tell me good night. I tried to think happy thoughts. I tried to picture myself having a good time at camp. I must have fallen asleep trying to come up with something positive. I ended up having a nightmare that a bear did come to camp after we all got there. Then a water main did break, but no one knew because we were so far away from the town it happened in. And soon enough we all started getting sick from drinking the water. Then a film director didn't come, but a news team did. They wanted to report on how seven campers were attacked by the bear and had to go to the hospital, and how everyone else at the camp was sick from the water. I woke up in a sweat. Why did I pray those terrible things?

"God, forget what I said!"

The next morning Mom came in to wake me up, and I reached for her and cried. She lay down beside me and held me. I was so mad at her for making me go, but I didn't want to stop hugging her.

Chapter 20

Mom drove me to my youth pastor's house and unloaded my bags to put in his van. Liza was already there. She showed me the shirt she was going to wear for the talent show; it looked a lot like the one I had packed. Mom gave me one last hug and talked to the youth pastor, Phil, about letting me call her if I needed to. He agreed. We waited for the other three kids who would be riding with us from church and then finally climbed into the van. The van door slid noisily on its rails and banged shut.

I was going to camp.

We played some Bible trivia for the first hour. I knew the answers to a lot of the questions but didn't feel like answering. About halfway there we stopped for lunch at a place that had three smaller versions of restaurants in a huge rest area. Everyone else ate their food and even got ice cream bars afterward. I didn't want to eat anything. We all hit the restrooms and loaded back into the van.

Thankfully I fell asleep for a while and didn't wake up until I heard the Australian lady on the GPS say, "In a half mile, turn right onto Gull Lake Road." I was no rocket scientist, but it didn't take a genius to figure out that we had to be very close since the place was called Gull Lake Family Ministry Camp. I felt the van slowing down and heard commotion outside. Our van was now following several other vans and cars. The vehicles were funneling through a mob of people holding posters and jumping around cheering. Phil rolled down all of our windows.

Happy, bouncing people in blue shirts were shouting, "Welcome to Gull Lake!" and, "We're glad you're here!" and, "Right this way!" As mad as I felt about being there, I couldn't help but smile a little bit. They all seemed so happy to have us come.

They motioned toward a parking spot and we pulled in. A tall guy with red hair opened our door and popped his head in. These people did not seem shy at all.

"Hi, guys! I'm Jase. Welcome to Gull Lake! What are your names?"

We each took a turn saying our names as we climbed out of the van. Jase high-fived everyone. Then a blond guy came up to Phil and held out his hand for the keys to the van.

"I'll take all of your things and unload everything in the pavilion up by the cottages. Go ahead to the Ministry Center and get checked in and sign up for your afternoon fun activities."

We all walked up a little hill toward the Ministry Center. You couldn't go more than a few feet without someone in a blue shirt high-fiving or fist-bumping you. A couple of the kids from our church had been there before and were attacked with hugs from people who must have met them in past years.

When we got to the front of the building, some girls were holding open the doors for us. "Welcome to the MC!" one of them said. "We're excited you're here!"

Why is everyone so excited for us to be here?

Inside the MC, a camp staffer put neon green bracelets on us that read *Gull Lake Ministries.* I noticed that all of the bracelets had a number on them. Liza and I both had a two on ours. We stopped off at several tables, getting a colored paper or signing something as we went, but always hearing, "We're so glad you're here!" or "Welcome!"

Are these people for real? I wondered.

The last table we came to had sign-ups for "Afternoon Fun" for each day of the week. The smile they had managed to put on my face vanished. I read through the options listed on the poster board. We could zip-line, get pulled on a banana float thing by a speeding boat, climb rock walls, or go on a "screamer swing." Oh, we could also shoot BB guns and a bow and arrows! No way was I signing up for any of that! I groaned inside. This was going to be the longest week of my life.

One of our church's youth leaders, Heather—Liza's mom—pointed to the sign-up sheets, then said, "Go ahead and sign up for whatever you want to do each day during free time!"

Everyone else walked over and started putting their names down. Except me. I spied a place called the Dock Shop and tapped Heather on the shoulder. "I'm going to walk across the hall and see what's in there while I think about what to sign up for."

She nodded and off I went. The outside of the shop had all kinds of colorful wooden plaques with inspirational sayings on them, like "Faith, Hope, and Love" and "In This House, We Believe."

I found a section with baskets full of colorful bracelets and headbands, and a table with striped blankets that had "Gull Lake Ministries" stitched on them. The rest of the shop had a bunch of racks with T-shirts and sweatshirts that all read "Gull Lake." I saw a T-shirt on the clearance rack that was a really cool green color with crackled white lettering. I actually wanted it, but wished it said something else. I wasn't sure I wanted to remember this place. Liza came in a second later with her mom. Just like that, Liza picked out a purple hoodie and Heather bought it for her.

"Did you want to get anything, Emily?" Heather asked. "You can pick up something now or come back another time."

"Another time," I answered.

She nodded and Liza said, "Well, let's go get our bags and check out our cottage, then! They should have everything unloaded by now."

We walked from the MC on a sidewalk, passing all kinds of cottages and condos. The girls from our church would be staying in the same cottage with Liza's mom. There were two sets of bunk beds in one bedroom, a single bed in another bedroom, a kitchen area, and a small living room. There were also two bathrooms. *Thank you, God!* At least I didn't have to walk out to a public bathroom where there could be strangers in the middle of the night, like at swim camp.

Once we got settled in, Heather suggested we head out. "Let's walk around, and we can show you all of the places you will be going this week."

This place was like its own little town. There were houses, a playground, a chapel, and all kinds of buildings for different things. It turned out that the MC had a gym, and the second floor had an indoor track that went all the way around and looked down on the gym, so you could walk or run and see what was going on below. There was even a bowling alley in there. Now that was a safe, fun thing I could handle.

The camp felt so big, I hoped I wouldn't get lost. I'd have to make sure I was with someone all the time so I would know where to go.

Heather led us to one last area. "This is going to be the most important place for you to know. It's where you will eat lunch and dinner, and it's right by the lake, where you'll probably spend a lot of afternoons."

As we got closer to the lake, I saw a huge, inflatable trampoline on the water. It was hard to miss, since it was bright yellow. Then I heard jet skis and boats speeding through the lake. On the beach I noticed some empty lounge chairs and a couple of little kids building a sandcastle using faded red buckets and plastic shovels. I looked back at the water and frowned. *No thanks on the trampoline and boats. Ditto on the rocky sand and seaweed-water.*

Liza piped up, "Shouldn't we head back to our cottage to get changed for dinner, Mom?"

"Good idea," Heather said, and we made our way back.

Each night the camp had a theme for dinner, and we were supposed to dress up for it. That meal's theme was the Olympics. I'd just brought a T-shirt that had "USA" and the flag on it. Then I discovered that Mom had also stashed a medal with a wide red-white-and-blue ribbon in my bag too.

I rolled my eyes and frumped my way to a bathroom to change.

Chapter 21

After we'd all gotten ready, we walked together, with different countries represented on our shirts, some wearing medals, some with headbands and face paint. A huge torch with a flame made out of some kind of blowing lightweight orange-and-red cloth stood at the entrance of the dining hall. The Olympic rings were mounted on the wall. Round tables filled the room, along with two big buffets, and I could hear the Olympic theme song playing over the speakers.

We found a table to sit at, and the guy in charge walked onto the stage and welcomed us—I guess just in case the 579 welcomes we'd already received weren't enough! He said his name was Ambush, which I thought seemed like an odd name. He told everyone about the week and then cleared the stage for a "Draw the Flag for the Country" game.

All of our tables had a stack of papers and markers on them. Ambush named a country and we had to try to draw the correct flag. Each table had to vote on the best flag from their group to go on to the next round. The winners from each table got to go on stage and compete in front of everyone. Heather won from our table and ended up winning second place for the whole contest. They gave her a medal made out of an oatmeal cream pie. Pretty clever.

After the game some camp workers pulled a blue banner across the whole front of the stage, and then a group of the guy counselors came running in, wearing white T-shirts, swimming trunks, and USA swim caps. They got up behind the banner and did a whole synchronized-swimming skit. They started out looking very serious and then made funny faces as they performed their different poses and stunts. It was hilarious! I laughed so hard I couldn't even control myself. It was one of those laughs where you just can't help sounding like a hyena having an asthma attack or a hungry pig with the hiccups.

The Olympic costumes that people came up with were pretty funny too. One guy was dressed in all white, with a turtleneck on and a sword. There were soccer players, people draped in flags, and some gymnasts.

The chicken parmesan we had for dinner was way better than Mom's, and there was gelato with Oreos crumbled on top for dessert. At least I could scratch starvation off my list of things to worry about that week.

As we finished eating, Ambush went back up on stage. "It's time for the counselor reveal!" He then took time to introduce all the staff and counselors and tell a little about them. Every counselor was a college student, from colleges all over the place. They all had nicknames that symbolized something about them—I figured that was why Ambush had introduced himself with such a unique name.

One of the counselors was Nancy Brew. She loved reading Nancy Drew books and also worked at a coffee shop. She was really pretty and seemed nice. Another counselor was called Short 'n Sweet. She was very short and worked in a candy store. She seemed nice too. Happy Feet was a dancer with long, red hair that she wore in braids. I wanted her to be my counselor. Maybe she would even have us dance. Justice League was a guy who played baseball and planned to be a lawyer some day. Happy Filmore liked to take videos of things and create movie projects. A bunch more were introduced before the last one: Fin Rider. He looked just like Flynn Rider from the movie *Tangled* and wanted to be a dolphin trainer.

The number on our bracelets matched up with the number of the counselor who would be our leader for the week. After they introduced themselves, they showed us their numbers so we could go off with them for some free time and to get to know each other. We were all told to do a drumroll by slapping the floor with our hands. Justice League hit a blow-up ball with a baseball bat. The kids that caught it held it up to show a number five on the ball. Kids shouted and cheered and made their way through the crowd to follow him out.

Happy Feet stood up next. Everyone started slapping the floor again. I crossed my fingers and hoped she had the sign for number two. She did a twirl and a leap and then danced around with a stuffed penguin. When she turned it around, it had a big number one on it. *Rats.* It would have been fun to talk about dance with her. All the number ones hopped up and followed Happy Feet outside. Nancy Brew came up next, wearing a detective hat. She held up a giant magnifying glass with a number two on it. She would be my counselor for the week.

All the number twos went off with Nancy to a grassy area outside the building. We were each given a small bag of Skittles, and then she gave us something we had to say for each of the colors in our bags before we could eat them. For our red Skittles we had to share something we loved to do. I told the group I loved to dance. For the orange Skittles we were supposed to share something about our families, and I said, "I have a mom, dad, little sister, two cats, and a dog."

The yellow Skittles were to share something we were proud of. I didn't know what to say. Some kids shared that they are good at playing an instrument or a sport. I was a big quitter in both of those categories. "I pass."

The green Skittles were to share what we were most looking forward to at camp. I wanted to say that I was most looking forward to going home, but instead I said,

"The talent show." It seemed like a normal answer to give.

Finally, the purple Skittles were to share personal prayer requests. If I listed all the things I needed prayer for, we would have been there until breakfast. *That I don't cry in front of everyone . . . That I don't break an arm or leg doing all the dangerous activities they have planned . . . That I don't make a fool of myself at the talent show . . . That I don't drown in the lake . . . And that I don't get attacked by a bear, bats, mosquitoes, or the boogeyman.* That would cover it for starters. "I would like prayers for a smooth start to middle school," I actually said. That seemed like a more normal thing to worry about.

Nancy told us we could go ahead back to our cabins and change into swimsuits. I was the last one to get up because I really didn't want to go in the lake. I didn't even like swimming in pools, so why would I want to go in a gigantic, deep, dirty lake?

Nancy called over to me. "Hey, Emily, I noticed you passed on saying something you're proud of. I bet there are lots of things you're good at. Can you name me one thing, just between us?"

I thought about it. "Well, aside from dancing, I'm really only good at one other thing, but it's not something I'm proud of."

"Can you tell me about it?"

"Worrying. I'm really good at worrying. Maybe the biggest worrier there is."

"Are you worried about being here at camp?"

I looked down at the ground and nodded. "Yeah, I'm pretty much worried about everything about camp."

"Hmm. Well, Miss Emily the Worrier, maybe we can turn you into Miss Emily the Prayer Warrior. Can I pray with you?"

I looked up at her and nodded. "Uh . . . sure."

I bowed my head, and Nancy put her hand on my shoulder and prayed for me: "Dear God, please wrap your loving arms around Emily right now and during her week at camp. Help her to know that through prayer, she can connect with you and know that everything will happen according to your perfect plan. Please bless her time here and help her experience your grace and peace as she enjoys learning more about you and fellowshipping with all of the awesome campers. May this be a transforming week, strengthening her faith in you and herself. Amen."

I opened my eyes and slowly brought my head up. It felt like Nancy already knew me.

"Emily, do you know Psalm 55:22? It says, 'Cast your burden upon the Lord and he will sustain you; he will never allow the righteous to be shaken.'"

I pursed my lips and gave a short nod. "I think I may have heard that one."

"Another favorite of mine is Philippians 4:6–7: 'Don't worry about anything; instead, pray about everything; tell God your needs, and don't forget to thank him for his answers. If you do this, you will experience

God's peace, which is far more wonderful than the human mind can understand. His peace will keep your thoughts and your hearts quiet and at rest as you trust in Christ Jesus.' And there's another verse about fear that I'll look up and share with you tomorrow. I can't remember the exact spot, but it's a really good one."

"Is it 2 Timothy 1:7? 'For God hath not given us the spirit of fear; but of power, and of love, and of a sound mind.'"

Nancy gasped and raised her hand up for a high five. "Yes! That's the one! I'm impressed, girl! You focus on those three verses and God'll do the rest. Everything will all work out. Now go get your swimsuit on and we can hang out at the lake."

I gave another nod but didn't like the idea of going into the water at all.

Chapter 22

I headed back to my cabin with all kinds of thoughts racing through my head. Surprisingly, my thoughts were not about the fish in the lake or the death trampoline. I couldn't stop smiling about Nancy. She knew I needed to talk, even though I hadn't even realized I'd wanted to. She prayed for me and the words came to her so easily. She knew by heart the exact verses I needed to hear. I'd been memorizing verses since first grade, but never really understood *why* it was so important to memorize them. Now I got it. If you had them tucked away like that, you could pull them out to use them to help yourself or other people on the spot. I decided I would try to memorize more verses so I could do that. And then I thought that it would be really cool to be a counselor someday when I was in college.

I got my suit on and was looking forward to talking with Nancy more. Soon enough I found Liza at the lake, and we hung out in the sand for a while. Someone on the other side of the lake unloaded a boat into the water and tossed a long, yellow, inflated banana float with handles in after it. A line of kids formed to ride the floating banana. It was pretty funny to watch. About eight kids could fit on there and the boat would race through the water while they screamed and laughed behind it. As soon as the boat turned, the banana would tip and toss everyone off. They all had life vests on, so everyone would just wait there, bobbing in the water until the banana came back again and then they could climb back on. After watching a couple groups ride the banana, Liza jumped up and begged me to go on it with her. A part of me started trying to figure out what could go wrong, but then I got up anyway and got in line with her. I started feeling excited about going on it. I wanted the next group's turn to end soon so I wouldn't lose this feeling.

When I got my life vest on, I shot up a quick prayer: *Lord, thank you for giving me Nancy as my counselor. Please keep me safe on this banana ride and help me be brave.* Then I climbed on and grabbed hold of my handle, squeezing my eyes shut. Within seconds we were going so fast that I couldn't close my mouth. It was a blast! Even when we all flew off of the thing, the vests kept us afloat and I didn't have to worry about the fish or choking on water. We just climbed back on and zipped around the lake again.

Afterward, we all changed out of our suits and Nancy took us hiking up this big hill. She wouldn't tell us where we were going or what we were doing. When we got to the top, I realized what was about to happen. We were zip-lining back down that hill. I was in such a good mood that I didn't want to ruin it by working myself up into freak-out mode. I started praying and remembered my verse from PJ: *God has not given me the spirit of fear, but of power. I have the power to not think about all the things that could go wrong. Lord, please help me be brave again and please be my life vest for this ride like you were for the banana float.*

I watched as the other kids got suited up and put on helmets. Nancy helped me get mine on. An instructor there was telling us how to grip the rope and how to hold our feet. We had to wear gloves too. Liza asked the instructor to take a picture of the two of us with our gear on. She was next in line. When she took off down the line, she screamed her head off.

I was next.

Everything looked so beautiful from up there. I couldn't help but feel God smiling down on me—brave me. They had me sit on the platform while I grasped the rope in a death grip. Then they gave me a little push. I screamed my head off just like Liza had. The wind whooshed my hair back as I zipped through the trees on the cable, taking it all in as I flew by. What a rush! I loosened my grip a little. I was going so fast and the ride was so smooth. When I got to the bottom, I hoped we would get to do it again tomorrow.

Nancy was the last one down. We stopped off at the Ministry Center and grabbed some popcorn seeds and a long-handled black popcorn popper. We all doused ourselves with bug spray and joined the other groups by a fire with a huge ring of logs around it. Some kids were roasting marshmallows; others were just sitting on the logs talking. We loaded our popcorn popper with seeds and took turns shaking it over the fire. It felt pretty heavy after holding it for a while. I took my turn first, then handed it off to Liza. Nancy told me a story about a girl from a few years ago who was scared to try the zip line. Every day they would hike up that big hill and she would say she was going to do it, but then she would change her mind when her turn came.

"She was more nervous than a long-tailed cat in a room full of rocking chairs!"

I laughed at the way she told the story. It did seem really silly to be scared when she could see that everyone was completely safe and having fun.

"The last day, she finally mustered up the courage to ride it. She loved it but was sad that she missed out on all those chances earlier in the week. That's why I—I mean, that's why *she* had to come back the next year and the next year and finally become a counselor. She didn't want to miss out on any of the fun again."

I stared at her. "*You* were the one afraid of the zip line?"

She gave a small smile. "Yep. Busted. I was the biggest chicken there ever was."

"Wow, I would've never guessed. You seem like you wouldn't worry about anything."

"Why do you think I memorized the perfect verses about worrying and trusting God? My dad shared those verses to help me, and then God used me to share them with you."

Just then Liza started yelling, "Nancy! Emily! The popcorn's going crazy! Do you have a bowl?"

Nancy ran over and helped Liza empty the popcorn into a blue plastic bowl. We doused it with salt, sat on a log together, and munched on it. Happy Filmore and Fin Rider were playing their guitars, and several of the kids in their groups started singing some praise songs. The fire was crackling, and the sun was setting across the lake. I couldn't imagine a better place to be at that moment. It was warm and beautiful and happy. I even felt warm and beautiful and happy on the inside.

By the time we went back to our cabins to change into our pajamas and brush our teeth, it was late. I was exhausted. We climbed into our bunks, and I grabbed Brownie out of my bag and started to pray. Before I knew it, the room was light again. The room was light! Liza's mom was telling us to hurry up and get to breakfast! I slept through the night in a strange place!

Chapter 23

I couldn't believe I had made it through the night. I didn't even get scared once. I didn't call my mom or cry or wake anyone up. I was so stinkin' proud of myself that I couldn't stop smiling. I went to breakfast with a whole new outlook on camp. I had some scrambled eggs with cheese, and also pancakes with strawberries and powdered sugar on top. Yum!

We started with break-out groups. We had a Bible lesson and then had time to practice for the talent show. After that it was craft time. I made a bracelet with colorful beads on it and the letters "GLSC," for Gull Lake Summer Camp. We had pizza for lunch and then we had discussion groups with our counselors. Nancy talked to us about the power of prayer. She didn't have to convince me. I was living proof.

After group time we had free time to play in the lake, rock climb, zip-line, or just hang out. I decided to try rock climbing first. The gear was a lot like what we had to wear for zip-lining. The rush wasn't about speeding down a hill, though. It was about carefully climbing to the top and ringing a bell up there. With God as my life vest, I made it up there and rang that bell as if I had the most important announcement to make to the world.

Then I went on the zip line again, and later even got in the lake and bounced off the trampoline into the water a bunch of times. This place was so much fun. A week didn't seem like enough time. Liza and I braided our hair and changed into the outfits we were going to wear for the talent show to practice one more time before dinner. It felt good to dance. Liza's energy and friendship made it even better.

Her mom called over to us. "You girls should take dance lessons in Demotte. Your mom and I could carpool together."

I couldn't believe it. "I would love that! I'll ask my mom for sure."

"Speaking of your mom, she sent me a text this morning checking on you. She was surprised she didn't hear from you last night. Were you supposed to call her?"

I smiled. "No, but I bet she thought I would. I was so tired I didn't really think about it."

We all went to the dining hall and had shrimp and baked potatoes. Then they brought out these tall glasses with layers of pudding and whipped cream and chocolate cake. It was delicious! With full bellies we headed to the Ministry Center and helped set up folding chairs for the talent show.

A girl named Jamie started out with some awesome yo-yo tricks. She had a really funny song in the background while she whipped that thing all around. She didn't mess up once. Then a brother and sister did a duet to the song "Amazing Grace." It was beautiful. Happy Filmore showed a stop-motion video he'd made that looked like a Lego guy was walking all by himself all over camp. It was hilarious! Fin Rider did some magic tricks with foam yellow bunnies. They were appearing and disappearing all over the place. Then it was Liza's and my turn to dance. A camp worker cued the music. We didn't miss a beat. We nailed it and had a lot of fun. When the song was over, it felt like ringing the bell at the top of the rock-climbing wall all over again.

That night was a lot like the night before. I was so tired that my head hit the pillow and I was out almost before I'd even started to pray. I woke up to Liza jabbing her mom's phone at my face.

"Your mom wants proof that you're alive, Emily. Wake up and talk to her!"

I laughed. "Hi, Mom."

"Emily? Are you having fun? I'm surprised you haven't called."

"Yeah! I'm having a great time! Sorry I didn't call. I've just been so tired by the time we come back to the cabin each night. This place is so awesome."

I could hear my mom sniffling.

"Mom? Are you upset I didn't call you?"

"No! I'm so happy that you're having fun. I'm so, so happy for you, honey!"

"Oh, well, I *am* having fun, and I'm sorry I was so mad at you for sending me. I'm not mad anymore. I wish I could stay longer."

"That's great, Em. I'll let you go. I'll see you this weekend. Love you!"

"Love you too, Mom. Oh, and there's something we need to talk about when I get home. Bye!"

Chapter 24

The last part of the week was as wonderful as the beginning. I made sure to stop off in the Dock Shop to buy that green Gull Lake shirt. I knew without a doubt that I wanted to remember this place. The only bad part was having to leave on the last day. Saying goodbye to Nancy was the hardest part of all.

"Emily, I'm giving you my email address so that you can write to me whenever you want. I can't wait to hear all about sixth grade. You'll have to let me know when you get Psalm 55:22 and Philippians 4:6–7 memorized. Then you get to give me two verses to learn."

I gave her a big hug and cried for the first time that week. "Thank you for everything, Nancy. You'll never know how much you helped me and how you made me feel. You made me forget about all my stupid worrying and reminded me to trust God."

"You were already a prayer warrior, Em. You just needed to truly trust your life vest."

We loaded up the van and headed back toward home. The trip seemed really short because I slept most of the way. My mom was there waiting when we pulled up. She gave me a big hug and was in a hurry to get me back home. She told me she had a surprise waiting for me.

When I got to my room, there sat a long turtle tank with a turtle swimming around in it. The first day I was at camp, a baby turtle had wandered up the grass from Grandpa's pond and he put him in a bucket to give to Mom.

Mom said she and Dad went right to the pet store and got a tank and filter and plants and everything he would need. By the third day he wasn't moving his back legs and wouldn't eat anymore. On the fourth day they didn't think he was going to make it, so they released him by a nearby creek. By some miracle my grandma called on the fifth day and said she found another baby turtle and asked Mom if she wanted it. She went out and got him, and he loved the tank and had been doing great. Grandma said God put him there just for me.

I was so excited to have my own turtle. I named him Gully, after Gull Lake. Mom asked me a million questions about camp. I showed her and Dad and Maddie the video of the talent show and told them all about the zip line and the rock climbing and the banana float. By the end of it, Maddie was begging to go to camp next summer.

"Maddie, you would love it!" I said. "I loved it so much that I want to be a camp counselor there someday. That way I can spend the whole summer at Gull Lake instead of just a week."

"What?" Maddie said. "You want to spend the whole summer away from home? You won't be scared?"

I shook my head. "Nope. Gull Lake's awesome. I loved it. Oh! I almost forgot. Mom, if Liza signs up for dance lessons in Demotte, can I sign up too? Her mom said we could take turns driving there."

My mom's face still had a look of shock on it, likely from me saying I wanted to spend the summer at camp.

"Mom! Did you hear me?"

"Uh . . . yes! Yes . . . we can work that out, I think. I'll call Liza's mom about it tomorrow. So, you really had a great experience, huh? I'm so glad."

"Yep, I can't wait to go back."

I put all my dirty clothes in the hamper and climbed into bed. I didn't check the locks or study any shadows. I just prayed and went to sleep.

The next day I got up and reminded Mom to call Liza's mom. While they were talking on the phone, Liza walked over to my house. She sat down on our porch swing by me, and I noticed that she looked kind of sad.

"Liza, did your mom say you couldn't take dance lessons?"

"No."

"Do you miss camp like me?

"No—well, yes, but that's not what's wrong."

"Then what's wrong?"

"I have to start school next week, and I forgot all about that until we got back from camp. What if none of my friends are in my class? There could be a lot of kids I don't know."

I held back a smile and put my hand on her shoulder. "Liza, I know exactly how you're feeling. It's gonna be okay. Do you know the verse Philippians 4:6–7?" I went to my room and grabbed my Bible off of my chair. During camp I had written out the two new verses from Nancy on note cards so I could memorize them. I came back out and sat on the porch swing again, then read the verse to Liza. "'Don't worry about anything; instead, pray about everything; tell God your needs, and don't forget to thank him for his answers. If you do this, you will experience God's peace, which is far more wonderful than the human mind can understand. His peace will keep your thoughts and your hearts quiet and at rest as you trust in Christ Jesus.'"

"I think I've read that one before."

"Why don't we try to work on memorizing it together? Nancy shared it with me when I was nervous about camp. It made all the difference. We can celebrate when we know it by going out for ice cream or something."

She smiled. "That sounds good. I'm glad we became closer at camp. To think, all these years we lived so close together and didn't hang out much."

Mom got off the phone and came out on the front porch. "Sounds like we're going to have a couple of dancers. It starts next Thursday. I'm going to get you there the first week, and Liza's mom is going to take you both there the next. I don't know why I didn't think of doing that sooner."

I side-hugged Liza. "It's settled then. Liza, we'll each try to memorize verse six by then and say it to each other on the way to class. Then we can do verse seven the next week."

"Deal!" she said.

Chapter 25

My friends all had appointments to get their nails and hair done for the Back-to-School Bash. Mom, though, refused to pay for that kind of stuff. "It isn't prom, Emily. What will you have to look forward to in high school if we do all of that now? Besides, I have a surprise for you that will give you a new look for the dance."

I didn't know what she could be talking about. Was I going to get a new haircut? High heels? A new dress? Maybe she *was* going to let me get my nails done. Nope. Mom did my nails for me and said she said she would curl my hair. She said I had to wear the dress I wore for my uncle's wedding, and I could wear the same shoes too.

"Then what's the surprise, Mom? Doesn't seem like there's anything left."

"You'll find out your surprise after eye therapy."

Eye therapy. *Great.* I had forgotten I had an appointment. It was an extra long one too because I was due for my annual exam afterward. At eye therapy they had me do all the usual kinds of weird eye exercises. I had to look at beads on a long string and tell them if they looked like they were doubling or if the string was making an X. I had to press buttons on a computer when I saw certain things on the screen, and I had to read all kinds of things. I couldn't wait until I was done with eye therapy. At least I only had to go once a month. Madison still had to go every other week. She'd even had to wear an eye patch for a few years. I guess I was lucky I didn't have to do that. It was bad enough having thick bifocal glasses.

After eye therapy I went downstairs to the exam room with Mom and went through all the normal eye-chart stuff. The doctor flipped the lights back on. "Your mom says that you can get contacts. Do you think you're ready to try some?"

"What?" I snapped my head around to face Mom and smiled. "I can get contacts? I thought you said I had to wait until I was a teenager."

Mom laughed and gave a nod.

"Yes!" I said to the doctor. "Yes, I'm ready to try them!"

The doctor chuckled and sent me to the back room to work with a lady who taught me how to put them in and get them out. The best news was that they let me take a month's trial supply home so I could start wearing them right away.

No manicure or hairdo or high heels could have topped this. I hugged Mom when I came out from the back room. This was such awesome news!

Chapter 26

I couldn't wait to get to the dance the next day to see everyone's reactions to seeing me without my glasses. All of my friends were excited about their new dresses and hairdos and nails; I was excited about my new face. For all these years I had been hidden behind my glasses and goggles. Now the contacts straightened my eye for me, and it felt good.

Dad dropped me off at school. "You look so grown up, Em."

"Thanks, Dad. I guess I grew up a lot this summer."

When I got to the school, some people didn't even recognize me! It was hilarious seeing people take second looks to see who I was. I felt beautiful.

I found Hailey right away. "Emily! You look so pretty!"

"Thanks! So do you. I like your dress."

Lauren walked up. "How was camp? We missed you at practice!"

"Camp was amazing. You wouldn't believe all the things I learned."

"So . . . way better than swim camp then, huh?" Hailey asked.

"Yes. No comparison."

"Oh, we need to get together sometime this week to get all our glow-in-the-dark stuff together for the Glow Run," Hailey said.

The music started playing and we all headed out to the gym floor to dance. All of my fears of locker combinations not working, getting lost in the new building, and even having time to pee between classes . . . it all seemed so silly now. Middle school was going to be fine.

Chapter 27

That Sunday in church I had tears in my eyes as we sang "Awesome God." *He certainly is!* I gave him extra thanks and praise for his grace and for blessing me with his gift of faith.

The ministry spotlight that morning was from our youth pastor, Phil. He told everyone about how the Gull Lake trip went and showed a short video of our time there. Dad put his arm around me, and Mom started crying.

Then Phil told the congregation about an upcoming mission trip to the border of Texas and Mexico. The team would go and visit an orphanage, help with painting and cleaning in the area, and spread God's Word. He said eight people had committed to go so far and asked if more wanted to sign up.

I looked over at my mom. She and Dad were holding hands and still smiling from the video. Maddie was drawing pictures in her journal, not paying attention to anything, as usual.

I couldn't believe the church was sending people there. Dad had watched police shows about how dangerous the Mexican border was. People were killed trying to cross over to make a better life for their families. That whole area was poor and full of so much crime. Our family even sponsored a little girl in Mexico. With every letter and update we got, I just wanted to cry for her. Then I remembered a verse we'd sent her on her Christmas card last year: "Be strong and courageous. Do not be afraid; do not be discouraged, for the Lord your God will be with you wherever you go," from Joshua 1:9.

Some of the words kept running through my mind. *Do not be afraid . . . God will be with you wherever you go.* I glanced over at my parents again. I put my hands on the back of the chair in front of me. I gripped the blue fabric. I watched a family stand up and raise their hands on the left side of the sanctuary. I saw no fear on their faces.

I shifted in my seat, still digging my fingernails into the top of the seat back in front of me. Mom looked over. Her face had a mix of surprise and worry as she looked into my eyes. I took a deep breath, glanced over at Dad, and then I stood up and raised my hand. "I want to sign up."

Afterword

This book is based on a true transformation my daughter Emily experienced the summer she learned to trust in God to overcome her fears and anxiety. Although some events and details are fictionalized, many of these scenes are right from our lives.

Emily really did go on that ministry trip to the border of Mexico and has also served on Skid Row in Los Angeles. She has a big faith and is finishing up her senior year at Grace College, where she is majoring in elementary education.

Emily went to Gull Lake Family Ministry Camp every year after that first summer. It became our family's vacation many times! I highly recommend it as a meaningful, fun place to spend a week of your summer with your family.

About the Author

Shannon Anderson has taught for 25 years, from first grade through college level. The highlight of her teaching career was being named one of the Top 10 Teachers who inspired the Today Show in 2019. Shannon is now a full-time author and national speaker. To learn more about her books or contact her to speak at your school or church, you can visit www.shannonisteaching.com.

Printed in the United States
by Baker & Taylor Publisher Services